Old Wives' Tales

The Iowa School of Letters Award for
Short Fiction

Prize money for the award is provided by a grant
from the Iowa Arts Council

OLD WIVES' TALES

Susan M. Dodd

University of Iowa Press Iowa City

The previously published stories in this collection are:

"Walls," *Epoch* (Summer 1983).
"Coelostat," *Ascent* (September 1983).
"Berkie," *Mss.* (Fall 1984).
"Wild Men of Borneo," *Crazyhorse* (Fall 1984).
"Rue," *Yankee* (November 1984).
"Browsing," *Tendril* (Fall 1984).

Library of Congress Cataloging in Publication Data

Dodd, Susan M., 1946–
   Old wives' tales.

   (The Iowa School of Letters award for short fiction)
   Contents: Rue — Coelostat — Public appearances — [etc.]
   I. Title.   II. Series.
PS3554.O31804   1984   813'.54   84-8879
ISBN 0-87745-132-X
ISBN 0-87745-133-8 (pbk.)

University of Iowa Press, Iowa City 52242

© 1984 by Susan M. Dodd. All rights reserved.

Printed in the United States of America

FOR MY FATHER

". . . praising a forehead called the moon
singing desire into begin . . ."
— e. e. cummings

Contents

1	Rue
25	Coelostat
43	Public Appearances
63	Wild Men of Borneo
75	One Hundred Years of Solicitude: The Meditations of Ursula
89	Walls
109	Potions
123	Snowbird
145	Berkie
171	Browsing

RUE

Miss Rainey Roth of Wyoming, Rhode Island, did not believe in luck. Sixty-one years old, a self-sufficient woman with a business of her own, she had no time for hazy notions. People who believed in sudden strokes of good fortune, she thought, were simply seeking an excuse for idleness. Nothing was apt to help a person who wouldn't help herself.

This sensible attitude was not the least bit undermined or shaken when, on the fifteenth of September, Miss Rainey discovered she had won ten thousand dollars in the State Lottery. She became a winner (the word seemed remarkably foolish, applied to herself) not through luck, but through carelessness: someone had dropped the ticket on the path to her small herb and spice shop. Miss Rainey had never bought a lottery ticket in her life, and she wasn't sure whether her practical nature or her whimsical streak prompted her to save the numbered stub, to check it against the winning numbers announced in the paper a few days later. Either way, she was sure of one thing: she wasn't about to let the benefits of a rather silly accident alter her realistic outlook. Luck, indeed. Luck was largely a matter of paying attention.

Miss Rainey was accustomed to making decisions. She rarely sought advice, made up her mind with an almost savage authority. On the day her winnings were confirmed, she remained in the potting shed behind her house, where she put up flavored vinegars and scented toilet waters, potpourris and pomander balls. The scents from the drying sheaves of lavender and comfrey and sweet basil cleared her head. By late afternoon, she knew precisely what she was going to do with the ten thousand dollars which had fallen so peculiarly into her lap:

She was going to keep her feet on the ground.

She was going to pay off the remainder of the business expansion loan she had taken out two years ago with the Wyoming branch of the Old Stone Bank of Providence (an outstanding balance of $3,764.25, according to her records).

And she was going to get herself a proper divorce. Legal. Official. Once and for all.

The following morning, Miss Rainey phoned the bank. Mr. Gencarella, the branch manager, sounded like a rejected suitor when she told him what she was about. He congratulated her, however, and agreed to make the necessary arrangements. Miss Rainey made one more phone call. Then, dressed in the gray tweed suit reserved for important business, she walked to the foot of her driveway. Her coarse, curly hair, still more black than gray, was tucked into a wool beret the color of wild chicory blossoms. A silk scarf of peacock feather print was loosely knotted at her throat. With a gray-gloved hand, she reversed a hand-painted wood sign. "Open for Business . . . kindly consider the well-being of resident cats and visiting children. Drive with Caution," was changed to "Closed." No excuses. No promises.

The private investigator's office was in a nondescript six-story building in downtown Providence, within sight of the State Capitol. After checking the directory in the dim, narrow lobby, Miss Rainey took the stairs to the third floor. There was an elevator, but she was not of a mind to wait for it. She needed to stretch her legs after the long drive. At the top of the stairs, she followed a sign shaped like a pointing hand: "Franklin R. Alfino, Room 302." It relieved her that the nature of Mr. Alfino's services was not specified on the sign or his door. She thought this boded well for his discretion. The floor of the short corridor, speckled marble, was wet, and amonia fumes made her eyes water. She passed three unmarked doors with pebbled glass windows before reaching Room 302.

Its door ajar, Room 302 was just that—a room. Perhaps fifteen feet square, windowless, uncarpeted. It contained one desk (gray metal), three file cabinets (one oak, two green metal), a small black safe, and a man in shirtsleeves who looked nearly as old as she was. Miss Rainey was taken aback.

"I beg your pardon, I should have knocked," she said.

The man looked up slowly from the newspaper spread across his desk. "No problem. Mrs. Roth?"

"Miss."

The man smiled. "Miss Roth. Come on in." He waved casually toward a rickety folding chair she had not noticed beside his desk. "Have a seat." He did not rise or fold his newspaper. "What can I do for you?"

Miss Rainey occupied the chair gingerly and with the utmost reluctance. She could already see she had made a mistake. The office itself did not disturb her, though it was certainly shabby and less than clean. Still, it was utilitarian, like her own workroom in the former potting shed.

The man, however, was nothing like herself. More to the point, he was nothing like what she had imagined. A private investigator should, to her way of thinking, look alert, energetic . . . perhaps a bit sly. Mr. Franklin Alfino looked innocent and slothful. His narrow shoulders seemed pulled down by a center of gravity located in his soft, round belly. He had very little chin, no hair to speak of, and his brown eyes, too close together, looked sleepy. He reminded her of a Rhode Island Red laying hen. She was hardly surprised when he cackled.

"Don't like my looks, huh?" He leaned back in his swivel chair and stretched, exposing a rumpled shirttail. "That's the chance you take with the Yellow Pages."

"I beg your pardon?"

"Isn't that how you found me—the Yellow Pages?"

"In fact it is," Miss Rainey said.

"Figures." Alfino nodded. "Started with the A's, right?"

Miss Rainey felt herself flushing, as if she were caught in some ill-considered fib.

"Don't tell me Paulie Abrams is all booked-up?"

The fact of the matter was that Miss Rainey had ruled out Paul C. Abrams because she found his ad distasteful. She could muster little confidence in professional services commended to her attention by a large India-ink eye with spiky lashes. Franklin R. Alfino had been the second name in the phone book, limited to a simple line-listing. She had thought, or hoped, this might indicate reliability, seriousness of purpose. His appearance in the flesh, however, did much to counteract that favorable first impression.

"I think perhaps . . . ."

"Looks aren't everything," Alfino said. "Mannix I ain't. But you could give me the benefit of the doubt."

"Mannix?" Miss Rainey fingered the soft leather strap of her handbag nervously.

"The T.V. glamour boys . . . weren't you expecting somebody like that?"

"I do *not* watch television, Mr. Alfino. Nor have I had occasion to require the services of a private investigator previously. I didn't know what to expect."

"Let me tell you something, then—free advice." Alfino was grinning, and the expression made him look a good deal less sleepy. "There's sixteen of us—private eyes—in Providence. Another five in Warwick. I know all these guys, and you can take my word for it—none of 'em look much better than I do. Fact is, you could do worse."

Miss Rainey said nothing for a moment, a doubtful and worried crease in her forehead. Finally, while Franklin Alfino continued to stare at her, she smiled. "Pretty is as pretty does," she said.

The detective cackled. "So what can I do for you, good lady?"

"I wish to locate my husband," Miss Rainey said.

"I thought you said it was 'miss.'"

"I prefer it. My husband and I have been . . . estranged for some time."

"Okay . . . miss. What happens then—when I find him, I mean?"

"I would like you to make whatever arrangements are necessary for him to divorce me."

"You want to get divorced?"

"I want," Miss Rainey said, calmly and distinctly, "for *him* to divorce *me*."

"But—."

"I am willing to pay."

Alfino shrugged. "How much?"

"We'll cross that bridge when we come to it. In the meantime, he must be located."

"Whatever you say. Name?"

"Lorraine Elizabeth Roth."

"His, I mean."

"John Amos Dudley."

Franklin Alfino scribbled in the margin of his newspaper with a ballpoint pen. Without looking up, he asked in a monotone, "When and where, to the best of your knowledge, was Mr. Amos last seen?"

"*Dudley*." Miss Rainey sighed. "Commander Dudley. Point Judith Pier. He sailed for Block Island. The bluefish were running. He never came back."

"So he may have drowned?"

"He did nothing of the kind."

"How do you know?"

"Because he wrote and told me so. A postcard. Of the Watch Hill carousel."

"Have you got this card?"

"Certainly not."

"Don't suppose it'd help much, anyway. He tell you where he was going?"

Miss Rainey sniffed. "'Where the spirit moved him,' he said." She saw Alfino trying to suppress a smile. "Even *I* had to be somewhat amused, Mr. Alfino."

Looking sheepish, the detective asked, "Why don't you call me Frank?"

"I'd rather not."

"I'm sorry?"

"Nothing to be sorry about," Miss Rainey said firmly. "I am simply not one for informality in business dealings."

Alfino studied her, and she saw she had been mistaken: his eyes were alert as a chicken hawk's.

"Back to business, then . . . Miss Roth. When did you receive this card?"

"I believe it was the first of July," Miss Rainey said.

"Postmarked—."

"The first of July, nineteen forty-three."

Franklin Alfino rubbed his eyes with his knuckles, as if he'd had cold water thrown in his face. "Ho, boy . . . ," he said.

"*You* can divorce *him*," her father's friend Judge Brimford had told her in nineteen forty-four, in his pleasant walnut-paneled study overlooking Narragansett Bay. "There is no earthly reason why you need ever set eyes on the scoundrel again, my dear." Rainey's father had recently died, and the Judge, retired, attempted to offer her *ad hoc* paternal advice and judicious affection.

Rainey had thanked the Judge and done nothing.

"*You* can divorce *him*," a Providence lawyer had pointed out in nineteen forty-six, when Rainey was buying the farm in Wyoming with the intention of beginning a new and independent life. "A legal notice is published. A brief wait. Then, if he doesn't appear—which we may assume he will not—the divorce is granted. *Pro forma.*"

"But *he* left *me*," Rainey said.

"Immaterial."

It was not immaterial to Rainey. She had thanked the lawyer and left.

"*You* can divorce *him*," Franklin Alfino told her now. "Much simpler."

"So I understand. That is not, however, what I want."

Alfino sighed. "Have it your way."

"I intend to," Miss Rainey replied. She did not leave until she had answered all the detective's questions and written him a check as a retainer.

Driving back to her farm, Miss Rainey Roth felt cautiously optimistic. Perhaps Franklin R. Alfino was unlikely to set the world on fire, but he knew how to take direction. And he was evidently not as befuddled as he looked. The hourly rate he proposed to charge for his services seemed reasonable. Besides, Miss Rainey didn't relish the prospect of another go at the Yellow Pages. The private investigators of greater Providence were probably not, as Alfino had suggested, a particularly congenial or impressive lot. Now that she had selected one, she might as well give him a chance, the benefit of the doubt.

Ten days later, Miss Rainey was arranging bittersweet and marsh grasses in lacquered Chinese baskets when she heard a car coming up the drive. Although her automotive knowledge was limited, she recognized the sound of a car in desperate need of a new muffler. She winced at the unwholesome racket upsetting the late morning calm, but kept on with her work. Footsteps scattered gravel on the path outside. She glanced through the small window and saw Franklin Alfino approaching the shop. She went out.

"You've found him?"

"Nothing yet. Sorry."

Miss Rainey tried to keep impatience from her tone. "What is it, then?"

"Had to come out this way, your neck of the woods. How about some lunch?"

"You want me to give you lunch?" she asked faintly.

Alfino tossed back his head and cackled, scaring off a squirrel from some nearby shrubbery. "I want to *take* you to lunch. There's a little tavern, not far . . . on the road to Exeter. How about it?"

Miss Rainey's usual lunch was a cup of sassafras or chamomile tea with saltines or a slice of buttered bread, and she frequently forgot to have that until three o'clock. She looked completely astonished at the detective's suggestion.

"Best cheeseburgers in Rhode Island. Chowder's homemade."

"I look a fright."

"Take off that smock thing and I wouldn't mind being seen with you." Alfino's eyes hooded sleepily. "Besides, I want to talk to you. Business," he said.

He drove more like a tourist than a detective—slow, aimless, his concentration adequate, but sporadic. Miss Rainey leaned back and looked out the window, waiting for him to speak. He did not. When he pulled up in front of the roadhouse—a place she had never visited, but assumed disreputable—she regretted the ride was over. The leaves were beginning to turn, and she realized that she always worked so hard at this time of the year that she scarcely had time to notice the colors of the season. "Bittersweet," she thought.

The Hilltop Tavern was as dilapidated inside as its exterior promised. The air was stale, smelling of beer, tobacco, cooking fat. Several men in work clothes sat at the bar, drinking and staring at a television screen high in a corner, suspended from the ceiling. Miss Rainey could see that they were watching an old horse opera. She thought she spotted John Wayne, huge, gravel-voiced, and very young. Alfino led her to a booth in the opposite corner of the room, and she chose the side of the table which placed her back to the television.

"Place doesn't look like much, does it?" Alfino said. The remark was offhand, but she got the feeling he was trying to gauge her reaction. She paused, pursing her lips.

"Pretty is as pretty does," she said at last.

The detective grinned. "Wait till the chowder—that's *beautiful*."

A stout middle-aged woman in a white nylon dress and an orange calico apron, who had been standing behind the bar watching television when they came in, approached the booth. "What can I get you?" No menu was on the table and none was offered.

"Chowder and a cheeseburger?" Alfino asked Miss Rainey.

"I believe just the chowder will do nicely, thank you."

He turned to the waitress, whose bored gaze was drifting back to John Wayne. "And bring the lady some johnnycakes, too. I'll have the chowder, onion rings, a burger medium-well, and a Narragansett draft. You want a beer?"

For a moment, Miss Rainey thought he was still addressing the waitress. "Oh . . . no, thank you."

"What'll you have to drink?"

"Tea?"

"Don't have it," the waitress said.

"Then a glass of water, please."

"You got any hard cider in yet?"

"Yup."

"Bring her one of those."

Miss Rainey opened her mouth to protest, but Franklin Alfino startled her speechless by reaching across the table and chucking her under the chin. "Trust me."

"That it?" the waitress asked.

"For now," Alfino said.

Miss Rainey waited until she felt sure the woman was out of hearing before she spoke. "Mr. Alfino—."

"I wish you wouldn't call me that." He sounded aggrieved.

"Please—."

"I know, I know . . . you don't believe in mixing business with pleasure." He hunched his shoulders and seemed to duck his rather large bald head. "But you did come out for lunch with me. How come?"

"I had nothing to offer you at home," Miss Rainey said.

Alfino raised his mournful eyes and smiled. "You're honest, I'll say that for you."

"I'm afraid I never learned not to be. I'm a very solitary person, Mr. Alfino. I've not had much need for tact and pleasantries."

"You went to college."

Miss Rainey felt accused by the flat statement. "That has nothing to do with it."

"Don't get your back up. I just meant you talk like a person with education."

"A young ladies' seminary. In Boston."

"A seminary . . . you mean like a priest? What, were you going to be a missionary or something?"

"A seminary was like a finishing school, Mr. Alfino."

"Yeah? Are you finished?"

She smiled.

"What'd they teach you there, on the level?"

"To speak like an educated person. Tact and pleasantries, too, I suppose . . . but I lacked the aptitude. Or have forgotten, perhaps."

"You're all right," the detective said. "Pleasant enough for me."

"Thank you." She felt flustered, like a schoolgirl.

"I'm going to college myself. Community college. Nights. Getting an associate's degree in accounting."

Miss Rainey blinked. "Why, that's very . . . commendable."

"Incredible, you mean." He laughed. "I'm sixty-four . . . don't ask."

"You look a good deal younger."

"Lady, you say you got no tact?"

Miss Rainey squirmed uncomfortably and the vinyl seat-padding under her squeaked. "You said we had business to discuss?"

Alfino's face resumed its somnolent expression. "I haven't been able to turn up a thing."

"So I gathered. I didn't expect this to be uncomplicated."

"Did you expect it to be expensive? Because I gotta tell you, the hours are mounting up."

Miss Rainey raised her chin. "I'll decide when I can no longer afford your services."

"Hey, don't get me wrong—I can use the work. But this could take months, and even then, it might be a blind alley. I'm just trying to be honest with you."

"Of course . . . ."

"I hate wasting your money, when it'd be so easy to get you a divorce without finding your . . . ."

"Husband," Miss Rainey said firmly. "I am still married to him."

"Sure. And you don't want to be—that I can understand. What I don't understand is—."

"You don't need to understand," she snapped.

The detective's nostrils and lips pinched, drawing together

as if a swift and shocking blow had been dealt to him. The waitress returned, and Miss Rainey looked away. Plates, bowls, and glasses were set on the black formica table with unnecessary clatter.

Miss Rainey felt sorely distressed by her unintentional sharpness. "I'm sorry," she murmured.

"You're right, though, it's none of my business—that part of it."

The waitress sauntered off again.

"I suppose that I *do* want you to understand." The admission was clearly difficult for her.

"Never mind. Try the cider."

"He left me, so he should divorce me . . . people must take responsibility for what they do."

"You loved him?"

Miss Rainey looked severely at Franklin Alfino and did not speak for a full minute. He waited, watching her face with eyes that were alert under half-lowered lids.

"I did," she said finally. "But what's important is that I promised myself to him. And John Amos Dudley promised himself to me. Whether I loved him is beside the point, Mr. Alfino. I would have kept my promise regardless. I *have* kept it, for thirty-nine years."

Alfino shrugged. "No disrespect . . . but what's divorce gonna get you now?"

"Very little, I suppose you might say. But I've reached an age where I don't care to leave loose ends."

Franklin Alfino picked up a dented soup spoon and stirred thick white chowder in a gray plastic bowl. Behind wisps of steam, his face was troubled. Miss Rainey reached for the pepper. Neither of them started eating.

"May I ask you a question . . . a personal question, Mr. Alfino?"

"Shoot."

"What makes you go to college? Do you intend to become an accountant?"

His cheeks seemed to sag when he smiled, and the dark pockets under his eyes deepened. "I'm a little old to start over." He picked up a greasy salt shaker and held it, right-side-up, over his soup. "But I'm not . . . 'finished.' There are certain things still interest me, things I'd like to understand . . . I never really had a chance to learn them until now."

"Precisely." Miss Rainey nodded. "I want John Amos Dudley to look me in the eye."

"You think if he does you'll understand something?"

"I rather doubt it."

"But you'd have a chance to try?"

"I believe we understand each other, Mr. Alfino."

The detective leaned across the table and gently tucked a paper napkin inside the high collar of Miss Rainey's blouse. The bristly back of his hand brushed her cheek. "Your johnnycakes are getting cold," he said. "Eat."

Several weeks passed with no word from Alfino. Miss Rainey was not surprised, but she was restless. She busied herself in the shop, preparing for the holiday trade. The second week in October, summer returned to New England. For four days, the sun beat down on the tin roof of the work shed, making it unbearably hot. Crickets chirped at night. The cats, Oleander and Hyssop, seemed stupefied.

Miss Rainey tried not to allow the extraordinary weather to disrupt her autumn routines. She packaged extra sage and thyme for Thanksgiving stuffing. She tied whole cloves and nutmeg, cinnamon stick and cardamom seed in tiny muslin sacks and designed a new label with instructions for "Wassail Bowl." When perspiration dripped into her eyes, she swiped impatiently at her brow with the back of her hand and thought how the heat would dry the herbs quickly, sealing in their flavors. She kept busy. She kept her feet on the ground. And she kept thinking of John Amos Dudley, who had courted her in a late Indian summer like this one, wed her the first week of Advent. Rainey had worn a silk shantung suit the color of champagne—it was wartime, Chantilly and satin were considered frivolous. Her bouquet of white tea roses was bordered with lavender and rosemary. Lavender for luck. And rosemary for remembrance.

John Amos Dudley was a local boy made good by war. A Lieutenant Commander in the Navy stationed at Quonset Point, he fought the enemy on paper. He was tight-lipped and clear-eyed when Rainey's father inquired about the specific nature of his duties.

Commander Dudley was a serious young man. Only Rainey Roth, with her high spirits and her quick tongue, could make him laugh in uniform. He was the son of a brakeman for the Providence and Worcester, and his family lived in a modest house near the railroad station in Westerly, Rhode Island. His mother had died of a stroke during the hurricane of '38, and his father's heart had failed the following year in a freightyard outside of Boston. John Amos was their only child.

Rainey met him at a tea dance at the Watch Hill Yacht Club on the last summer weekend of 1942. His dress whites were impeccably tailored and pressed and his eyes were the color of the hazy horizon over Montauk. They waltzed—something by Victor Herbert, she recalled—and the plum-colored sleeves of Rainey's afternoon gown had fluttered in three-quarter time against the uncompromising white of Commander Dudley's shoulders.

Now, the extraordinary warmth and fragrance of Indian summer revived her whirlwind romance, her scant months as a wife—continuing to live with her widowed father in the large, shingled house on the pond at Haversham, while John angled for weekend leave. She had still felt like a bride, when the bridegroom vanished, abandoning her and the war effort and the United States Navy, for bluefish and Block Island and the spirit that moved him.

'The spirit that moved him'—even now, nearly four decades later, Miss Rainey realized that she lacked the frailest notion what such a spirit might have been. On their wedding night, in a large cherry spool bed in the guest room at Haversham (her father had considerately gone fishing with Judge Brimford immediately following the ceremony), John had wept in her arms, confessing his longing to be a warrior of the sea. He had petitioned to be sent to the South Pacific, attached to a cruiser or battleship. The Navy's continued refusal to make him a hero perplexed and unmanned him. Rainey had stroked his wet cheeks, reassuring him of his manliness, secretly hoping to conceive a son as the proof her husband needed.

By late spring, John Amos Dudley had his assurances: he received orders to join a heavy cruiser in the Aleutian Islands and Rainey was carrying his child. In June, three days before he was to ship out, he sailed in a rented skiff toward Block Island, alone, with fishing gear borrowed from Rainey's father. Weeks later, when the Watch Hill postcard had come, Dr. Roth had quietly paid the owner of the skiff and purchased new fishing tackle. Rainey, at three and a half months, had miscarried the child she had been so certain was a son. She understood that the man to whom she had promised herself was a coward. Beyond that, however, "the spirit that moved him" eluded her.

It was this, the mysteriousness of John Amos Dudley's spirit, that most tormented Rainey. The yearning to see her husband's face once more was not prompted by passion or bitterness. Those, like the humiliation, had passed. But she could not abide knowing her life had been shaped and confined by something whose nature she failed so totally to grasp. And she supposed she wanted her husband to look her in the eye, to renounce her outright, because she still cherished a hope that she might yet make a man of him.

For a time, government men had come to the house at Haversham, full of probing questions about the Lieutenant Commander who disappeared. Rainey and her father were both shamed by the accusations implicit in their questions and their flat, official eyes. But there was nothing to hide. When she received the picture postcard of the Watch Hill carousel (a New York postmark), Rainey had relinquished it to her government gladly. Her aging father, retired from medical practice, had been gentle, noncommittal, eager to avoid his daughter's gaze. He did not live to see the end of the war, and Rainey felt her disgrace shortened his life. In her innocence, she had consorted with the enemy.

Now, as the sun beat down on the tin roof, Miss Rainey Roth twisted stalks of marjoram into Advent wreaths, inhaled the heady smells of dill and basil and oregano, and looked back on the chapter of her life whose ending she would finally be able to write, thanks to a numbered chance carelessly dropped on her garden path. She fashioned nosegays of strawflowers to adorn the doorways of fussy women with cheerful, orderly families. She filled them out with sprigs of eucalyptus for scent. Rosemary for remembrance. And she waited to hear from Franklin R. Alfino, Private Investigator.

The odd, misplaced hot-spell passed and autumn returned. Now the air had teeth in it. Miss Rainey removed her woolen cardigans from the cedar chest in the attic and hung them outdoors to let the wind lessen the pungent odor of southernwood. On cold mornings, she plugged in a small electric heater in her workroom. She massaged her stiff fingers with warmed camphor oil at night.

It was a chilly overcast morning, and she was standing with her back to the heater, pasting hand-lettered labels on bottles of pale pink chive blossom vinegar, when Franklin Alfino returned. She did not hear him approach until he opened the door, setting her Japanese glass windchimes clashing.

"Good Heavens!" A handful of bright paper squares flew from her hands and floated to the floor.

The detective squatted awkwardly and began to gather up the scattered labels. "Scare you? Sorry."

"Startle a body out of her wits," Miss Rainey muttered.

Alfino straightened up and gave her a mildly reproving look.

"Don't mind me," she said.

"Get up on the wrong side of the bed?"

"It's getting up that matters." She tried to sound businesslike. "Have you something to report . . . or do you just happen to be 'in my neck of the woods' again?"

"Got anything around the house for lunch?"

"It's ten o'clock in the morning, Mr. Alfino."

The detective smiled good-naturedly. "I learned how to tell time at detective school, Miss Roth. Got any coffee?" He looked pointedly at an electric percolator on the corner of her workbench. It was plugged into an extension cord which reached, just barely, to an outlet halfway around the room.

"Herb tea. I do not approve of coffee."

"Don't know what you're missing. I'll settle for anything warm, though . . . even if it tastes like boiled socks."

Miss Rainey brewed tea in a tarnished copper kettle she took from the windowsill and placed it on the table along with two chipped earthenware mugs. Alfino cleared a space among the litter of vinegar bottles, labels, and glass cannisters of loose herbs. Without speaking, they sat side by side on the two rickety chairs which had once belonged to the austere dining room at Haversham. Miss Rainey took the mug without a handle and the chair with a loose hind leg.

"This isn't so bad," Alfino said.

"Lemon verbena, the herb of enchantment."

"You putting a spell on me?"

"I might try, if I thought for a moment it would get you down to business."

Alfino bowed deferentially. "All you gotta do is ask, good lady."

Miss Rainey's hands, trembling slightly, closed around her spotted brown mug. "I am asking," she said.

"I've found him."

"Where?"

"I don't know how to say this tactfully."

"Never mind that. Where is he?"

"In New Bedford. In a cemetery."

Miss Rainey Roth stared at Franklin Alfino. Her eyes, glistening with anger, were fiercely blue. "He's dead?"

"Almost fifteen years. I'm sorry . . . ."

Her lips flattened out in a hard, straight line.

"Maybe it's just as well," Alfino said uncertainly.

Miss Rainey replied slowly, in a choked voice. "It simply is not . . . acceptable." She started to get up. Then, without warning, her mouth framing a small silent "o" of distress, she slumped to the floor in a dead faint.

She awoke on the horsehair sofa in her own front parlor. The air was musty, for the room was unused and unloved. Her father's fine furniture surrounded her, dusty and unforgiving. Franklin Alfino bent over her, covering her with his raincoat, a rumpled tan thing she had noticed when he first arrived: at last, something about him seemed to fall in with his occupation.

Miss Rainey came to like a person taking charge of a small emergency. "Don't fuss. I'm fine." When she sat up, too quickly, the color drained from her face. She dropped back against the sofa cushions. "I'm perfectly all right."

The detective wrapped the soiled sleeves of his coat around her shoulders. "Now, just take it easy for a few minutes."

"I never faint . . . must be coming down with something."

"A shock. Want some water?"

"What happened to him?"

"Your—."

"Husband," Miss Rainey said firmly.

"We'll talk about that later." Alfino looked uneasily around the cold, formal room. "Nice place you've got."

"We'll talk about it now, Mr. Alfino."

"You ought to—."

"Now," she repeated.

Alfino sighed. "Seems he drank himself to death. Put in a State institution in '65, died within a year. He was buried there. No living relatives, he told 'em."

Miss Rainey closed her eyes, nodding weakly.

"You sure you're all right?"

"He never even looked me in the eye." She turned her face to the rough, stern sofa-back, and the detective realized that she was weeping.

"It's finished," he said softly. "You're rid of him."

"No," she whispered. "I am not."

The following week, Miss Rainey sent a sizable check to Franklin R. Alfino, Private Investigator, for services rendered. She was free of debt, and nearly a thousand dollars were left from her Lottery winnings. Her feet were on the ground, her business was unencumbered, her unfortunate past dead and buried. She tried to summon up satisfaction over the loose ends snipped from her life, and she kept about her work. In her herb garden, only the rue—that bitter shrub symbolizing repentance and said to restore second sight—remained green. She cut it back, pausing to bruise a handful of leaves and rub their oil on her forehead, for her head often ached. The Four Thieves . . . blind Adam . . . the Pharisees . . . it was a poor company she joined, anointing herself with rue.

The shop was doing a brisker business than in previous years. People seemed more interested in caring for themselves properly. Miss Rainey expanded her stock, devised more appealing labels and packaging, lectured at the town library and the Women's Club on the healing properties of common herbs. Exhausted at the end of each day, she took herself off to bed and courted sleep with hops tea and an inventory of her blessings. She was, after all, independent, content.

Something, however, had come over Miss Rainey Roth of Wyoming, Rhode Island. Mary Alice Potter, the town librarian, marked the change. So did Mr. Gencarella at the bank. Miss Rainey looked well enough, but her step seemed slightly less determined, her shoulders less straight. When she addressed the Friends of the Library, her ideas did not seem quite so "definite," Mary Alice said. The lines in her face were deeper, yet softer too, as if sorrow had won a victory over disapproval.

In short, Miss Rainey had been widowed.

The first Sunday of Advent was bitingly cold. A furious wind lashed the last leaves from the trees and brought small branches down with them. Wearing a severe black gabardine coat which had hung in the back of her closet for a dozen years, Miss Rainey went to the foot of her driveway, turned over her sign, and drove to New Bedford, Massachusetts, the port from which the stern Captain Ahab had pursued his great white nemesis.

She had called Franklin Alfino the day before for directions to the hospital. At first, he had refused to give them to her.

"What do you want to do that for?" he said. "Let the past stay buried."

"This is *my* concern," Miss Rainey told him.

"Mine, too."

"Why should you make it your business?"

"Like I told you, good lady, some things still interest me."

In the end, however, Alfino had given the directions and even offered to accompany her. Miss Rainey had turned him down with unaccustomed gentleness. "I must do this myself. It's between me and—."

"Your husband," he said. "I understand." The detective sounded sad and old.

"Franklin?"

"I thought you didn't want to call me that."

"Our business is finished now," Miss Rainey said.

The State hospital was located to the west of the city, several miles off a straight, little-used highway. The cemetery, Alfino had told her, was to the left of the main gate, behind a grove of pines.

Miss Rainey was stopped at the gate. She rolled down the car window and informed the elderly guard that she merely intended to visit the cemetery. He told her where to park and waved her on without curiosity, pulling a plaid muffler over his jaw.

There were no other visitors in the graveyard, a small square tract of land made monotonous with rows of plain markers. Miss Rainey had no trouble finding the plot she wanted. It was identified by a gray granite slab the size of a dress box: J. A. Dudley, 1917-1966.

Wind tore through the trees. There was faint music from a nearby hospital building, but it could be heard only when the wind paused. The strains were brassy, but too sporadic for her to recognize. Miss Rainey stood beside the grave of her late husband, studying the two lines of letters and numbers meant to memorialize him, and trying to recall his face.

But even now, John Amos Dudley refused to look her in the eye. The face of the young Lieutenant Commander was darkly tarnished and dim, and the forty-nine-year-old drunkard buried here was unimaginable to her. Only a dazzling white sleeve and the color of the sky over Montauk came back to her. Miss Rainey waited. Behind the brutal wind, she thought she detected a waltz. But even as she listened, she knew she was making it up . . . as deftly as she had made up the contentment of her life.

When the breeze abated, the music made itself plain. A march—John Philip Sousa, if she wasn't mistaken. The false heartiness of parades and toy soldiers. Miss Rainey straightened her shoulders and gave a little shake of her head. Then she opened her handbag to remove a small pouch of unbleached muslin.

The dried herbs, mixed that morning, were comfortably rough and familiar to her fingers, something known and understood. She shook them from the sack, cupping them in the palm of her right hand. Then, when the wind picked up again, she tossed the handful of earth-toned bits and pieces into the swells of air. They flew from her hand and seemed to rise over her head before they dropped unevenly upon the final resting place of her estranged and long-gone husband:

> Rosemary for remembrance . . .
> Thyme for courage . . .
> And rue, the herb of grace.

COELOSTAT

My mother earned her first, and last, American currency as a stenographer at the Nuremberg Trials. She spent most of the next twenty-three years at Maplecrest Psychiatric Hospital, interpreting atrocities in four languages. She had a talent for simultaneous translation. And an eye for detail. And almost total recall. Sometimes I wonder if I am really her daughter at all.

Such wondering is, of course, a petty luxury, bought and paid for by my mother's confinement, but I never could take it very far. I was brought up short the first Sunday of every month of my formative years. Visiting Day. I am my mother's spitting image. My doubts, like debts, were wiped off the books the first of each month: I paid. Her face, pared down by suffering to its lowest common denominator, confirmed our blood tie.

I called my father Dennis. That was his idea. Perhaps he realized from the outset he could not be both mother and father to me, although that was, strictly speaking, his assignment. Dennis was defeated by all of it—the mothering, the fathering, the strictness. Even the speaking was hard on him. He was a man of action, a perpetual First Lieutenant and a natural-born adjutant. But making the best of duty he wasn't cut out for, he rose to the challenge of my existence, treating me like a buddy and answering to me as Dennis. My mother's name was Hedwig. Dennis called her Heddy.

Names were important in our family, since both my parents were orphans and only children. My mother was orphaned by war, her parents buried somewhere beneath the rubble of downtown Dresden. Dennis was set on his own two feet by a crackling blaze on the Christmas tree farm in Kansas where he almost grew up. His parents went up in smoke while Europe was doing the same. Their only-begotten had just reached enlistment age. My grandparents' sense of timing offset their lack of staying power.

And so it was that Dennis and Heddy, disinherited before

reaching majority, were left only names to carry on. They split the difference between them, christening me Brigid Hilde for the ashes of my two grandmothers. Dennis, with his natural bent for cheerfulness, was soon calling me Buddie, so that before I was old enough to articulate objections, that was how I came to be known. I remain to this day Buddie Keoughan. "Buddie" is, in my opinion, rather unsuitable for a grown woman. But the same might be said of me.

I was educated in certain codes of behavior by my parents: spit and polish by my father, rape and pillage by my mother. These might be regarded as dubious legacies, I suppose, but since great pains were taken to hand them down to me, it is my duty to act as conservator. I am meticulous in my personal habits and inclined to the grotesque in my inner life. My premises are clean, my fantasies dirty. I presume this sort of thing often comes of mixed marriages.

I was barely two when Heddy went to Maplecrest. Her absence redesigned the contours of my existence. Suddenly I, accustomed to a bare-boned cage, found myself in a padded embrace. Motherlove had perforated me with sharp edges, teaching me baby evasions and caution. But the "nurse" Dennis hired as starchy substitute for Heddy was a great soothing loaf of a woman with a yeasty odor and a lap like a porch swing. My surrogate keeper carried horehound drops up her sleeve and a name unlikely to complicate matters further: Mary Parsons. Mary stayed with us, a soft and simple comfort, until I was nine. By the time she was too old to work, I was just old enough to look after myself. Timing is everything.

The winter Mary left, my father developed a sudden passion for celestial navigation. Without my motherly intermediary, I was highly susceptible to paternal fascinations, easily enlisted in his schemes.

A few items salvaged from the Christmas tree fire were stored in our attic. One January evening, when the house still seemed empty without Mary's bulk, Dennis carried a brass telescope and an old mantle clock downstairs to the kitchen. Both were black, but after a week's scrubbing with every sort of abrasive we could concoct, most of the soot and scorching were gone. Dennis had removed the clock's inner workings with surgical concentration and care, discarding the casing. On Saturday morning we went to the hardware store and purchased a variety of rods, tubing, and hinges, vials of screws, and a round piece of mirror. Finally, the whole collection was returned to the attic, where my father, working from his own sketches, devised an elaborate instrument for scanning the sky.

The night he finished, Dennis's face was pale and glistening, as if he had caught something from the stars.

"Look, Buddie," he whispered. "Isn't it amazing?"

I looked eagerly into the telescope's eye and saw reflected in the mirror only a swatch of the same frigid sky that was visible through the attic window.

I was at a loss for the praise he seemed to expect. "It's so you can see the sky," I said.

"Yes. But always the same part of it. Always the very same place, no matter how the earth turns."

"What's it called again?"

"Coelostat, honey. SELL-UH-STAT." He spelled the word for me, running his forefinger through the dust on the top of an old footlocker.

I studied the springs and angles and joints for a moment. The brass and glass gleamed under the dim attic light. Then my father unscrewed the hanging light bulb and put us in darkness. The clockworks ticked. "Amazing," I said, late with my cue.

Dennis disregarded me. "I did it," he said. His voice was hushed, the way it was when he spoke to me at Mass. "I don't even understand how it works myself. Not really. But I did it."

"Just like in the book," I said.

I leaned up against my father's shoulder in the dark, careful to keep my weight on my own feet. He put his arm around me, and his workshirt smelled of smoke and pine.

"Unbelievable," said Dennis.

I did not reply. I was trying to imagine what wonder he found in isolating a piece of something whose very endlessness was a miracle. It was my first inkling that my father and I were not of a single mind.

Dennis was pure Catholic, both by upbringing and by instinct. Tidy doctrines appealed to him. He believed, for instance, that the age of reason was seven. It reinforced his general sense of the rightness of things that my seventh birthday should happen to fall on the first Sunday of the month. On that day I was inserted into a new pair of patent leather shoes and a pink organdy dress with a smocked bosom, all spit and polish. I was, at seven, to be initiated into the rites of Visiting Day. The month was June.

A few weeks earlier, I had made my First Holy Communion: spit and polish and white. Reacquaintance with my mother in such close succession to this event seemed sacramental. Leaps of wisdom, bounds of grace. Confirmation.

It was a momentous occasion. Although I hadn't even scant recollection of Heddy (my psychiatrist disputes this, of course), I had been nagging Dennis to take me to Maplecrest. I resented exclusion from the mystery defined for me by the monthly shining of the Studebaker, the removal of the best suit from its zippered bag, the Deluxe Whitman's Sampler carried away unopened. For years my buddy Dennis had been attending a Sabbath ceremony without me. The age of reason dawned in the nick of time: I was growing bitter.

"*What are you saying? Kindly speak less fast.*"

These were my mother's first words to me. Then she smiled

a shifty underling's smile and let her eyes glance off mine. I had not spoken. But I obviously displeased her. "Please," she said sternly, "what *are* you saying?"

Her beauty came as a nasty shock. I was conscious for the first time of the cutting-edge of loss; it left me sensitive to nuance. All along I had presumed that something commonplace had been mislaid, my mother would turn up eventually. But her loveliness alerted me that a fine and rare belonging of my very own had been confiscated.

Her chin and cheekbones were mine. Her hair and eyes and voice were silver: cold and precious. My mother sat before an impregnable window, the hexagonal design of chicken wire embedded in the glass. She wore a heavy brocade wrapper, magenta, the color of entrails and penitence. She kept to a wheelchair because she no longer cared to walk. She kept to dim rooms because she had lost her taste for light. Her petal earlobes were pierced with garnets. She wore her wedding ring backwards, on the wrong finger of the wrong hand.

Spitting image: I resembled her the way a postcard resembles a Wonder of the World. The cutting-edge of loss . . . I turned small and flat and overcolored in her shadow.

I was a good loser. I held up straight and silent before my mother, my party dress and new shoes dulling as I was berated for lack of consideration, mumbling, and unspeakable crimes against humanity. Dennis rested his hand on my shoulder, inanimate as a paperweight. But my father's touch was not necessary to keep me from blowing away in the storm of my mother's disapproval. I had already confessed, prepared myself to receive. My Act of Contrition stood me in good stead. I kept my bearing, head tilted slightly back, lips parted. I met my maker with ready-made repentance.

"Heddy—," Dennis tried, like a buddy, to deflect her wrath from me.

"Americans!" my mother hissed.

Spitting image . . . I nodded, anxious to align myself with her.

"Quiet!" Her fingers moved rapidly, flying over the invisible keys on her lap. "*Please.*"

"We mustn't allow Mrs. Keoughan to become overwrought," the matron said. She clearly disapproved of my presence. Perhaps she was not a Catholic. Or she may simply have failed to see I had reached the age of reason. I was small for my age.

"Clear the court immediately," my mother commanded, heavy artillery and air raid sirens implicit in her voice.

The matron responded to authority by reflex, hustling Dennis and me into the corridor. When I looked back from the doorway at my mother, her fingers were scrawling a frantic shorthand on her knees. The Whitman's Sampler made a golden rectangle at the foot of her bed; restraints dangled from the iron headboard, awaiting a motion of adjournment.

Dennis had explained to me many times, with incremental linguistic complexity as years passed, that "Mommy" was not well. (He called her Mommy when he remembered to. But usually Heddy.)

"Heddy is away for a rest," he would say. "Mommy is resting." I learned to enunciate *sotto voce*, to glide *en pointe*. I developed an innate horror of all manner of disturbances, acquired an artistic sensibility: my tastes ran to the still life, the soothing landscapes of the Barbizon school.

"You okay, Buddie?" Dennis asked, as we drove out through the Maplecrest gate that first day.

I nodded, reluctant to gamble on sentence or appeal. The pink smocking was an iron band around my chest.

"Mommy is—."

"Resting," I said, to spare him.

"Yes. And I'll bet she remembers you better the next time."
I looked out the car window at the forsythia which flanked the hospital fence. There were black iron spikes rising from among the yellow and green branches. "She won't like me, Dennis."

"Oh, Buddie . . . it isn't *you*, honey. Mommy is . . . not well. You know. I've told you that."

"She's beautiful, isn't she?"

Dennis sighed. "Yes," he said at last. "Yes, she is. You are, too, honey."

Good Catholics make bad liars. My father could keep nothing from me. I knew then what I know now: I would always lack my mother's authority.

With this realization dawned the age of reason, flawlessly timed.

I do not believe my mother ever came to enjoy my visits. But she did come to accept them eventually, or seemed to. She stopped condemning me in any language I could understand, addressing me in low, gutteral syllables, while Dennis stood erect and slightly apart, an impeccable attaché.

Girl talk: Heddy's skeletal fingers ranged over chair arms and lap robes and bedcovers. She resumed, to the best of her ability, my tutelage. She wrote volumes on her atrophied thighs for me.

I was born in 1950 in Minneapolis. My mother, a lapsed linguist, died in 1975 in Maplecrest Psychiatric Hospital. I was her sole mourner and heir. My father, a veteran, died in 1974 in a Ford Pinto. I was baptized Brigid Hilde in tribute to my antecedents, called Buddie in compensation for my mother's chronic absenteeism. As a Catholic, I received on First Fridays. As a daughter, I was received on First Sundays. I have a B.A. in European History from the University of Minnesota and a fondness for chocolates with cream and nut centers. I believe in moderation.

These are the facts of my life. My psychiatrist tells me there are many more I overlook. He says, for example, that I did not have a normal upbringing. However, I fail to find my early circumstances irregular. One's experience with upbringings is necessarily limited.

There is more to my past, of course. More birthdays, more coming to grips with coming of age. The age of reason obviously does not descend all of a piece. Like any child, I had a daily existence to traverse, markers to reach on school transcripts, doctors' scales, social indices. Puberty caught up with me, like reason, piecemeal. I fulfilled, in common sequence, the basic requirements of growing up.

If I pass lightly over the details, it is not because they fail to interest me. On the contrary. At night I sift through my past like a beachcomber with the day's finds. My background, my origins, fascinate me. That is why I retain a psychiatrist: to keep my self-fascination within polite bounds, to avoid boring others with my past.

And my present? It is, regrettably, less riveting. This is why I have acquired a lover: to avoid boring myself with my present.

Yes, I have a lover. A married lover. How unlike me to commit what is so widely acknowledged as sin. But there was little choice involved. My mother's beauty turned on me, and my precocious flash of insight was accurate: I have never taken on the patina of authority. So it was not surprising, when I reached the age for a lover, to find no glut of candidates. Berger arrived in an open field, take-him-or-leave-him. I took him.

I met Berger at Maplecrest on Visiting Day. But he is no Rochester-figure, hopelessly mad wife in state-subsidized attic. And I myself was not in the hospital on my Sunday-best behavior for a digital chat with Mom. Through a twist of something less chancey than fate, I managed to become employed, not long after being orphaned, as Maplecrest's Director of Public Relations and Education. Berger is a psychiatric social worker. We were thrown together by our mutual affinity for the unsound.

Berger works at Maplecrest only on weekends. He has a full-time job during the week at a family counseling center in St. Paul. A second income became incumbent upon him when his twin sons reached college age. Berger subdues the unruly and soothes the anxiety-prone in order to pay identical tuitions at Dartmouth, a place he has never seen—and thus, is not precluded from visualizing as the medieval towers of Graz.

It was his voice that seduced me. I am abashed at my shallowness, but there it is. Berger was born and schooled in Austria, and twenty years in America have lessened his accent only by degrees. The first time I heard him speak, my inner ear closed snugly around his throaty syllables the way a baby's fist encloses a favorite rattle. His diction, awkward and precise, bowled me over with primal longings.

Our paths first crossed over a failed suicide. The patient, a member of Berger's Saturday morning therapy group, had tried to escape by setting fire to his own bathrobe. This gesture (Berger called it "a statement") was made on a Saturday night, in the third-floor patients' lounge, during a well-attended James Bond movie. This was not Mr. L'Heureux's first attempt to shape his own fate, but it was undoubtedly his most effective. The fire department had to be called in. This involvement of "outside authority," along with the subject's growing interest in involving his fellows in his future plans, forced me to request a conference with his family and his therapist on Sunday afternoon.

The immediate attraction I felt toward the middle-aged, melancholy-eyed social worker was an unforeseen complication. To counteract it, I conducted the meeting with every cool and deliberate mannerism I could recall. I must have been convincing in this stance, because the session was concluded quickly and to the evident satisfaction of all parties.

Berger stayed on after the survivor's distraught wife, son, and daughter-in-law had departed. "May I say that you have managed this delicate matter most admirably?" he said.

Working in tandem, we had convinced the family that a facility with "more security" would serve the patient's best interests. But the therapist and I, both having had opportunities to inspect such facilities firsthand, knew better. With the uninitiated gone, we felt the uneasy intimacy of conspirators.

"I have had some experience with these things," I said, haughty with inexperience.

"I certainly did not mean to impugn your credentials, Miss Keoughan." His Germanic pronounciation of my Gaelic name made it scarcely recognizable to me, and I smiled. "I intended simply to compliment you. Forgive me if the expression was . . . graceless."

"Mr.—?"

"Lutsdorf," he said, bowing slightly. "Berger Lutsdorf."

"Forgive me, Mr. Lutsdorf. I'm afraid I'm tired. No need to take it out on you."

"I understand. And you, you understand also—that I meant no offense?"

"Of course."

The tall, fair man in the wrinkled corduroy jacket studied my face for a moment. I felt exposed, as if his eyes penetrated into private recesses I knew were unfit to be seen. I gathered my files self-consciously and started for the door. "Thank you for your . . . support, Mr. Lutsdorf."

Berger Lutsdorf stepped after me, persistent. "I wonder, why is it we have not met earlier, Miss Keoughan?"

"I haven't worked here very long, actually."
"Then this excellent experience of yours was acquired elsewhere?" He had a compelling, uneven smile. His teeth had been neglected.
"No," I admitted.
"Then I am afraid I do not—."
"I was referring to personal experience." I quickened my pace down the hallway, a pale green tunnel.
He kept pace with me. "I have said something indelicate again."
I shook my head.
"Suicide?" he asked.
"Families," I said. "Kin of the hopeless. My mother died here recently."
"I see. I am sorry."
"Don't be. It was what she wanted."
"No one *wants* to die, Miss Keoughan."
"Sometimes it's the only viable alternative."
I felt a certain pleasure in my clipped reply, but when I glanced at Berger Lutsdorf, he looked sad and disappointed.
"You are remarkably clinical," he said.
The familiar gutterals of disapproval made me lower my head.
"Miss Keoughan, may I invite you to my office for coffee?"
I raised my chin and smiled brashly. "I imagine mine's bigger," I said.
"Your coffee?"
"My office."
Berger shook his head. "You Americans . . . ." Dove-colored hair fluttered above his thick platinum eyebrows. "Mine, Miss Keoughan, happens to be Viennese . . . if you would care to consider quality rather than size."
"Your office?"

"My coffee. I believe you will find it quite fine." He bit his lower lip, and I imagined my tongue removing the traces of cinnamon and heavy cream from the corners of his mouth.

"I'll just check in with the switchboard," I said.

The weekend after we formally met, Berger and I were meeting informally in the employee parking area. We sat in his Audi, although my Buick was bigger. Berger has taught me to appreciate quality.

I suppose our kissing had the same territorial motives which cause dogs to sniff and circle. But its hazardous impropriety endowed it, for me, with hints of higher purpose. I do not distinguish easily between the sacred and the profane. I leave such detail to Berger, who has philosophical leanings. I also entrust logistics to him. By the third weekend, we had driven out of the parking lot to kiss in earnest in my single bed across a border of white eyelet.

Berger's wife, whom I have yet to see, became an overnight irrelevancy. I doubt I'll ever regard her as an issue, unless she should take to disrupting our Sunday nights. She hasn't done so in nearly three years, though, except when major holidays and the birthdays of immediate relatives arise. On these occasions, I am leniently inclined: I, too, would be demanding about attendance at family celebrations.

I presented myself to my lover under false pretenses: I told him my name was Hilde. Berger accepted this and he still does. I feel my German name creates a certain bond. The deception is easy to maintain, since everyone at the hospital calls me Ms. Keoughan.

The appearance of a lover has lent my life purpose. I set about, from the start, to lure him with my mother's tragic start and finish, feeling none of the guilt I was geared for. In a way, it has been a comfort, finding this way to make Heddy's life finally useful.

COELOSTAT

Berger's eyes go soft and runny and rich, like fine Brie, whenever I allude to my past. I have taken pains to dole it out sparingly. Nuremberg stretches between my Hapsburg lover and me, unvoiced and unexplored, lending us a poignancy to which we are not really entitled. Sometimes our liaison seems a simple two-way reparation, with love both awarded and extracted. Of course, it is not simple. Or fair. But it does, finally, make up for something.

"I luff you." Berger said it after knowing me a scant three weeks. I said nothing, which he interpreted as pathos. Professional training has misled him to confuse discretion with anguish. He is capable of mistaking sealed lips for scars.

"I luff you," he said. In bed he whispers to me in German I must assume is flawless, my mother tongue having been cut out at an early age. Berger's passion, like classical music, is enhanced by a demanding form.

I have yet to tell Berger that I love him. I believe I do, but I cannot trust myself to speak with authority. Besides, there is pleasure in all withholding. So I remain mute, and my lover remains alive on hope and a gently misguided sympathy.

Berger leaves my bed at six-forty-five on Monday mornings. His wife, Elise, is under the impression that he works all night at Maplecrest, then goes directly to his job in St. Paul. Her willing belief is based on economic necessity, I suppose. I remain in bed while my lover dresses for his other life. He always tucks me in and sprinkles me with gutteral tenderness as he departs, locking my door behind him. Monday is my day off, Sunday being a strain for the orchestrator of relations between this public and the privately anguished. I often stay in bed nearly all day.

I have never been troubled by insomnia. This is not to say I am better adjusted than the average person, only that my maladjustments take forms other than wakefulness. I sleep the sleep of the undisturbed. Only since Berger has occupied my bed, however, have I discovered my aptitude for dreaming. The psychiatrist points out, predictably, that I've been dreaming all along. Perhaps. But if that's so, my lover has activated memory: in his wake the dreams are recalled. His voice has endowed me with retentive capacity.

I hoard my dreams in a locked box under the bed, where I can have access to them. Written in a spiral notebook. Coveted by my psychiatrist. I believe I see in my dreams the authority which I myself have always lacked.

My lover is no luxury, no mere self-indulgence. Berger has pulled together my past and my present. He is my biographer, approaching my hidden meanings with skills of immediacy and order. My sinful lover, giving subtitles to my foreign dreams, subduing my night-visions with his tough, lean limbs and agile fingers. Tender treatment. My lover: I will readily confess him, but I cannot regret him. And renunciation is beyond comprehending. Unlike Mommy, I am not multilingual. I have a single fluency. Berger's tutoring helps me to maintain it. He is the guardian of my small proficiency.

I am forced, ultimately, to pull away from the bed on Mondays, for I see my psychiatrist at five o'clock. A fashionable hour for running off to meet a man. My psychiatrist is more attentive than a moonlighting lover can afford to be.

In his frosted beige office, like a rich woman's hair, I speak the language accepted by the host country and understood in conventional alliances. The psychiatrist furnishes his opulent treaty room as a place where I can be magnanimous toward my defeated past. Unlike my lover, the doctor is wily, an able negotiator with a glib mouth and an acute ear. It is a challenge to maintain an embargo on my present against him. I outmaneuver him with ostentation, though, squandering my fifty minutes on the past. As if I had all the time in the world.

COELOSTAT

When the psychiatrist finishes with me, I go to a restaurant to eat something leafy or rootlike. I cannot bear the odors of meat and milk. On Monday evenings, I crave texture, and chew fried potatoes, oiled greens. Then I go to the movies. If the picture is any good at all, I am more susceptible to its suggestions than those of either psychiatrist or lover. Even the previews of coming attractions can be cautionary, supplemental, for there may be no dreams to tide me over through the rest of the week.

Life could, I suppose, be hard if I let it. There is a meagre quality to my existence. I am an orphan. An only child. I have a genetic bent toward conflagration. There is only one tongue at my disposal, and it isn't always what it should be.

Naturally, I take preventive measures. I will not drive a Pinto or dwell upon the horrors of war. I have never been to Europe, am unlikely to go, and I refuse to have a Christmas tree, unless it is artificial and has been treated with flame retardant.

I own up to my idiosyncracies: I am predisposed toward mental anguish, Teutonic manners, and men in uniform. I harbour a fundamental skepticism where Freudian analysis is concerned.

I have my reasons.

I have my doubts.

I have verbal proficiencies somewhat better than average, and I earn my living by them.

I have a married lover, as well. And questions to keep me occupied: I wonder, for instance, how I shall keep this married lover of mine, once the tuitions are paid? I wonder if my lover's wife might be talked or tricked into bearing another child to be expensively educated? Or if I could summon up the accidental courage to foist my own spitting image upon the world?

But that would be high crime. Reverse genocide. When I look at it that way, a married lover seems a simple sin, almost venial, if unoriginal. Besides, my lover's marriage is hardly my fault.

And I mean no harm, so far. All I ask is a recollection, a dream now and then. A remnant from which I can fashion something useful or decorative . . . or at least attempt to. Everyone, after all, is entitled to confirmation.

Excess absorption with one's antecedents is a common sort of coddling, but one I can hardly afford. I try to get by without it most of the time. My present is accounted for. And as far as the future goes, I feel I can be relied upon to know what to do when the time comes.

That is one of the advantages to a strong sense of timing: you needn't waste time looking ahead. You can simply stay where you are and wait, not worrying about what can't be changed. If you focus your eye on the same point long enough, it's possible to overlook the infinity surrounding it.

PUBLIC APPEARANCES

PUBLIC APPEARANCES

The Governor's wife thought the Governor was looking especially well this evening. As she stood before the mirror in the hotel suite bedroom, fastening her pearls, he appeared next to her in the gilt frame. The force of his presence, more than the width of his shoulders, shifted her into the lower corner of the composition. She became a detail.

"How do I look, do you think?" the Governor asked his wife.

"You're looking especially well this evening," she said.

The Governor nodded into the mirror.

The Governor's wife had taken particular pains with her own appearance. She knew this was an important occasion, although she could not remember precisely what or why. Something to do with the Governor's campaign—kickoff, victory—she had trouble keeping them straight. One campaign bled into another, like the lines in Madras cloth. Odd, she thought, that nobody else seemed to notice this.

"They cut my hair too short," the Governor muttered.

"Oh, no," she said. He needed her before major public appearances. "It's just right," she said.

"It doesn't look plastic?" His hair had turned silver, although he was still young. It called attention to the boyishness of his face.

"Plastic? Not a bit. It's perfect." The Governor's wife smiled at her husband, trying to reassure him. The mirror served as intermediary for their eyes.

"I was afraid of that. I hate it when my hair looks perfect."

She moved further into her bevelled corner. "I didn't mean it that way. I only meant it looks just . . . right."

The Governor sighed, squinted at his image and carefully disarranged the front of his hair. "Better?"

"Just . . . fine," she said. He needed her.

The Governor's wife slipped out of the frame. She felt worried. It seemed to her, now, that she had not taken enough

45

trouble with her own appearance: she was a disappointment. Downstairs the great banquet hall would already be filling with people who wanted a look at her. There would be photographers. She had read somewhere that certain tribes of Indians never permitted themselves to be photographed, convinced that the camera captured the spirit and bore it off. The Governor's wife understood this belief. She frequently stared at imprecise gray and black images of herself in the morning paper and felt horrified at her own lifelessness. Her husband, she thought, must be of a different tribe. The flashes and shutters enlivened and enlarged him. He acquired a natural glossiness in public.

She edged back into the mirror to glance at her hair. Because the occasion was important to her husband, she had gone to a beauty salon, her own hair a responsibility she couldn't manage. The dryer, a fierce metal helmet, was lowered on her for forty minutes; it gave her a headache and burned her ears. When they were finished with her, she thought her head looked lopsided and oversized, as if she had borrowed it. Her husband preferred her hair, unlike his own, to look perfect. It did not.

Still worried, the Governor's wife turned her attention to her dress. She wished the mirror allowed her skirt to be seen, but the frame cut her off at the waist. Although she was wearing the best dress she had, she suspected it wasn't good enough. She turned and went into the bathroom, shutting the door behind her without a sound.

It was bad luck, worse than walking under a ladder, to see herself in fluorescent lighting before important occasions. The uncompromising illumination was a bad omen, a hex on her morale. But the full-length mirror on the bathroom door persuaded her to risk exposure to the unlucky light. She turned to face her reflection and inspect her dress.

It was finer than any dress she had ever owned, not counting her wedding gown. It was made of real silk, the color of winter wheat, and it had cost more than a hundred dollars. She had gone to New York to buy it, so that her husband and his constituents would be unlikely to learn the details of her extravagance. It was the one and only time she had crossed state lines to commit an indiscretion. The money she spent was her own, a birthday check from her parents. But that didn't excuse her. She told her husband the dress was a bargain. He said, very nice. The first time she wore it, an important occasion last year, the Commissioner of Motor Vehicles had burned a hole in her skirt with his cigar while she was dancing with him.

The Governor's wife had mourned her dress for a full year, keeping it in a scented garment bag in the back of her closet. It was a shameful secret, the small charred perforation like an evil eye on her lap. She wore the dress in her dreams, which admitted no flaws or superstitions. She danced in it. Awake, she grieved irreparably.

Finally, two weeks ago, she had taken the ruined dress to a seamstress who was said to be a wizard. The old Hungarian woman, Magda Bogner, had consoled the Governor's wife with her shiny pins and deft hands. "I make like new," she promised. "Nobody even guess." Her throaty voice and thick accent suggested the unassailable authority of a fortuneteller to the Governor's wife, who rather believed in magic. It was a belief her parents had encouraged in her as a child. She had learned in adulthood to call it by other names and, eventually, not to mention it. But the belief itself was intact.

Mrs. Bogner had detached the skirt from the bodice, excised a narrow strip from it, and reassembled the garment with tiny stitches. When the Governor's wife returned for her dress, the burn was gone, like magic. She and the old seamstress had embraced in mutual delight at the fitting. For the first time in a year, the Governor's wife felt like dancing. The older woman considered her own dexterity commonplace. But the Governor's wife was sure there were rhapsodies and gypsy spells in the clever aged fingers. Impulsively, she touched them with her own, and the seamstress smiled at her, as if confirming a suspicion.

No money changed hands. Mrs. Bogner would not hear of it. "My honor," she said, "to do for you. I tell my grandchildren—I sew for wife of Governor. Maybe someday President." For a moment, the Governor's wife turned pale. When she recovered herself, she planned how she'd invite the needlewoman to the Executive Mansion for tea. Sometime when the Governor was out of town.

Now, the Governor's wife stared into the hotel bathroom mirror and reexamined the dress. It was fine, a perfect fit. The gypsy fortune held up under scrutiny: no one would ever guess. But the dress was not like new. The rustle of silk when she moved was not quite as gay or generous as it once had been. Magic no longer clung to her skirt. The Governor's wife switched off the harsh overhead light and returned to the bedroom.

The Governor had remained in front of the mirror, but now he was looking over the notes for his speech. They were typed in capital letters on buff-colored index cards. He looked up as his wife reentered the room, and she smiled at him hopefully.

"You're sure I look all right?" he asked.

They went downstairs a half-hour later than they were expected. Impact, he said, was largely a matter of timing.

There were twelve hundred people in the convention center banquet hall. Or so the Governor's press secretary had told the Governor's wife, who had cultivated the sensible habit of accepting the word of staff members on such matters. Nevertheless, tonight, as she was plunged into the crowd, she found herself wondering how many people were really there—exactly

PUBLIC APPEARANCES

how many. Twelve hundred and six, perhaps? Or maybe less than a thousand? She couldn't guess. She would never know.

There were certain things the Governor's wife had come to accept. Never knowing was one. Entering banquet halls by way of service elevators and institutional kitchens was another. She had learned to anticipate sudden explosions of light and sound when she followed her husband over thresholds. Experience had taught her not to wear rings on her right hand and to carry small purses with shoulder straps when she was placed in receiving lines. She willed herself to develop tolerance for embraces and personal questions from total strangers. She had a whole bag of tricks for remembering names and faces. She had her smile down to a science.

The Governor's wife frequently went out in public holding hands with younger men, something the Governor himself had suggested and even arranged. His wife was not "a natural," not even "a quick study." During his first campaign, staff members had tactfully brought it to his attention that his wife, who was small and rather timid, had an unfortunate proclivity for getting lost. Or *looking* lost, which was worse. The matter was discussed frankly—the Governor believed in treating staff like family. Eventually, it was decided that an aide should be assigned to the Governor's wife in crowds. The solution proved sensible. It was good training for the junior assistants. And the crowds, looking at the Governor, never seemed to notice the succession of pin-striped young men to whose hands the Governor's wife clung in public. Over the years, the handholding and her own determination not to slow her husband down had helped her to mask her misplaced look. In fact, she had acquired a small following of her own. Underdogs, particularly, looked up to her.

Now, flanked by aides, the Governor was moving briskly into the packed hall. The crowd parted for him, but closed quickly over his wake so that the young man holding the Governor's wife's hand had to fight to make a path for her. As always, the first moment of entering a crowd made the Governor's wife feel she was drowning. Hands grasped at her husband. Some of them, missing him, closed around her, as if she might be a rung by which to reach him. Yearning for air, she smiled and tightened her grip on the only familiar fingers she could reach.

"Kevin?" She said the boy's name to calm herself, as a stocky man shouldered his way between them.

"We won't lose him," the young aide reassured her grimly. His face was creased by the pressure of responsibility. He was twenty-three years old, and this was his first job. The Governor's wife wanted to tell him it would be all right.

"You are so skinny!" a lady in purple chiffon exclaimed, filling a momentary gap in the crowd. She pressed the Governor's wife to her bosom, where yards of violet fabric struggled against moist flesh. "I wish I looked like you. I'm going to send you a coffee cake."

The Governor's wife moved her lips graciously, knowing her voice was useless in the noisy room.

The woman turned to throw herself on the Governor. "Your wife needs to put some meat on her bones."

"She works too hard," he said, pulling his wife forward and circling her with his arm as he smiled into a bank of cameras. She lost her balance for a moment, and leaned against him.

"One more picture, Governor . . . this way . . . ." Her husband was pulled away and Kevin stepped smartly into the intervening space, providing equilibrium.

The dais was raised six feet above the floor, a head table of more than twenty places. The over-starched tablecloths, crudely mended in a random design, hung down low in front so that the feet of the dignitaries would not be exposed to public scrutiny. The Governor's wife, taking her place, kept her knees pressed together anyway. Whenever she accompanied her husband on platforms, she had a feeling that people could see up her dress.

Each place at the head table was set with heavy white dishes and dented cutlery. On each dinner plate, under a napkin folded like a fan, was a program with her husband's likeness on the cover. It was his official portrait, for which he had worn an expression she found forbidding. Above his head, embossed in gold lettering, it said, "Favorite Son." Each time she ran across the phrase, she wondered how it made the Governor's brother, a periodontist, feel.

"Handsome program," the Governor's wife said, but her husband did not hear her. He was going over his notes. She turned to her other side and smiled at the Majority Leader of the State Senate, who smiled back and said something she could not hear.

The Senate Majority Leader was in love with her. The Governor's wife didn't realize this, and the Governor didn't, either. In fact, the Senator was hardly aware of it himself. He was, after all, a happily married man with four children. An able politician. A hard-working legislator. He had a law practice to maintain, in addition to his legislative duties and family obligations. His star, the state's major papers all predicted, was on the rise. But none of this precluded the Senate Majority Leader from being a bit in love with the Governor's wife. He had fallen in love with her, slowly and surely, over a period of years, over a series of daises and platforms and lecturns and podia. The Governor's wife had a fragile, wounded look which attracted the Senate Majority Leader powerfully. He had not declared himself; he never would. He genuinely cherished his own wife and family, the law, and his rising star. But the Senator could not keep his eyes off the Governor's wife. He had no appetite when she sat beside him at head tables. He witnessed her fear and bravery across oceans of smoke and sweaty faces and watered drinks, and he wished that he could adopt her.

Tonight he was seated especially close to her at the center of the over-subscribed banquet table. Although their elbows were only inches apart, an arrangement of red and white carnations with miniature silk flags sprouting from them like unseemly pistils made a barrier between them. The Senator leaned around the flowers.

"You look very beautiful," he said.

The Governor's wife, picking the pleats in her napkin, looked up with startled eyes.

"A lovely dress."

Her smile wavered with pleasure, surprise, and disapproval. "Thank you." It was the most personal thing she had ever said to him.

At her right, the Governor speared a fragment of canned pineapple from his fruit cup as he looked over his notes. His wife turned to him as if he had spoken to her. The Majority Leader, who was Master of Ceremonies for the evening, picked up his own notes. This was an important occasion for him, too, a good opportunity for exposure. He had no business thinking about the Governor's wife.

How thin she is, thought the wife of the Lieutenant Governor, leaning forward from her chair at the far end of the table. Cool and thin and above it all and that dress must have cost an arm and a leg. Some people have everything. And she promised herself then and there that she would be better at it, better at all of it, than this Governor's wife. Her own time was coming, her place in the middle. She noticed that the Governor had begun to eat and she picked up her spoon.

A sour cream coffee cake, the lady in purple said to herself. With apples and walnuts. Vinny can deliver it in his cab. There was a vacant place next to her at the table. No one was looking. She quickly exchanged her empty sherbet glass for the extra one and began to eat the fruit. Hundred dollars a plate, damned if she wasn't entitled. Anyway, at least she had a good table, a clear view of the Governor and all them. Thin as a rail, that wife of his . . . no wonder. Look how she picked at her food.

At the rear of the hall, the Governor's staff had gathered at the bar. They knew better than to eat—canned fruit, rubber chicken, chemical ice cream. Everything according to schedule so far. The Governor's press secretary relaxed, sipping his first Scotch of the evening. His suit was rumpled and there were deep circles under his eyes. No one ever believed he was not yet forty: he was a veteran.

"Not a bad crowd," he said.

"Better than we thought, anyway," the speechwriter answered, taking a notebook from his pocket, pausing, then putting it back again.

"How many, you think?"

"Nine-fifty?" The speechwriter's guess was wary. Estimating crowds was not one of his talents.

"Close." The press secretary smiled enigmatically, trying to convince the junior assistants that he knew more than round figures.

"All the papers here?" the executive assistant asked.

"Every last one, the buggers."

"The networks?"

"Present and accounted for."

"Good. We've reeled 'em in. Now let's just hope the old man puts on a show."

"Don't worry, he will." Smiling again, the press secretary turned to the junior assistant assigned to the Governor's wife. "How is *she* , by the way?"

Kevin pushed his horn-rimmed glasses higher on the bridge of his patrician nose. "Seems fine."

"Knock wood."

At the note of derision in the older man's voice, Kevin turned and asked the bartender for a Coke. Then, noticing the press secretary's sardonic expression, he abruptly changed his order to a beer. An attitude of disrespect for the Governor's wife was something he took personally. Besides, he could not understand it. She was very kind to him, and he was proud that he could look after her. Several years earlier, however, while Kevin was still studying political science at Princeton, the Governor's wife had fled from the press corps. On two separate occasions. Her blatant panic had caused talk. The more experienced staff members had kept uneasy eyes on her ever since, regarding her as a problem which might crop up any second if they weren't on their toes.

"She looks good," the Governor's personal secretary said with a grimace of envy. "Nice dress." Her own dress, a plain navy knit, had been pulling across her hips since seven-thirty that morning. She had never made it back to her apartment to change. Retyping his damn note cards. She wondered if she had time, now, to dash to the ladies room and put on some make-up before the speeches got underway. Probably. On the other hand, another vodka might put more color in her face.

The press secretary was staring at her speculatively. "I don't know . . . ," he said.

"Whaddya mean?"

"The dress."

"Hers? It's beautiful . . . what's wrong with it?"

"Maybe a little too . . . rich."

"Shit, she's the Governor's wife! If I were the Governor's wife, I'd sure as hell wear rich clothes. I'd buy out Saks."

The press secretary laughed. "Then you wouldn't be his wife for long, sweetheart."

"Christ, they're serving slower than usual tonight . . . ." The Governor's secretary was still squinting at the wheat-colored blur beside her boss on the dais. Everything must look different from up there, she thought.

"Time flies when you're having—."

"Think dinner's slow, wait 'til the speeches start," the press secretary said, aiming a razor-sharp grin at the speechwriter.

Up on the platform, the Governor's wife abandoned her modest pretenses of eating. She had an irrepressible dread of being kissed, questioned, or photographed with her mouth full. To her left, the Majority Leader jotted a note on the back of his placecard. To her right, the Governor studied his speech. The Governor's wife gazed out over the huge hall and smiled vaguely toward the bandstand, where an awkward transition from "Yankee Doodle Dandy" to "Happy Days Are Here Again" was in progress. She could hardly wait for "Goodnight, Ladies."

"*Governor, Lieutenant Governor, Other Distinguished Guests at the Dais, Reverend Clergy, Ladies and Gentlemen, and Fellow—.*"

The Majority Leader's vibrant voice competed confidently with the clatter of coffee cups and dessert plates. The Governor's wife looked down. A block of red, white, and blue ice cream was melting to a lavender pool before her. She pushed the dish aside and sipped her coffee.

"Should I start with a joke, do you think?" her husband whispered.

"*He has done right by us and he has done us proud . . . we have given him our votes and our trust, and he has given us his all . . . we have—.*"

"A joke, yes. They always like it when you start with a joke."

"How about the preacher and the farmer—that one?"

"Oh, that's a wonderful story."

"Some of them have heard it before . . . listen, do I look all right?"

"*So we come here tonight, my friends, to say thank-you, Governor . . . we come here to say well-done, Governor . . . we come here, in short, to—.*"

"You look wonderful. Just straighten your tie a bit."

"*Ladies and Gentlemen, it is my honor and my privilege to present to you our distinguished Governor, our dear friend and our favorite son, The Honorable—.*"

The crowd, bellowing and stamping and clapping, lumbered to its feet like a bull. Smiling, the Governor began to move toward the podium. Then, pausing, a look of boyish embarrassment on his face, he leaned down to kiss his wife. The roaring and stamping intensified. The Governor's wife smiled shyly and applauded her husband along with the others.

"*My friends—.*"

For a moment, the public address system emitted a piercing whine. Without missing a beat, the Governor adjusted his tone and the angle of the microphone to a perfect balance.

"*A few minutes ago, my lovely wife suggested to me that I begin by telling you a joke—a joke that is a particular favorite of hers . . . .*"

The Governor's wife lowered her gaze to her lap, where her right hand, naked without the opal ring her parents had given her for her twenty-first birthday, lay on a silk field of winter wheat. Her fingers looked bluish, slightly swollen with too much handling.

"*But then, I said to myself—and those of you who know me know how rarely I disregard my wife's advice—but I thought, no . . . this is no time for a joke.*"

The folds of her skirt fell gently open as she sat. The Governor's wife could see the tiny hand-sewn seam where the scorched silk had been cut from her once-perfect dress. Nobody else would notice, it was true. But she knew: there was no longer an allowance in the skirt for gypsy magic, for dream-dancing. The dress was *not* like new anymore. The fullness of luxury had been trimmed from it.

". . . *no jokes tonight, my friends, for this is to me a solemn occasion . . . . Yes, we have a victory to celebrate . . . and yes, we have another campaign ahead . . . but in this interlude between them, we face . . . .*"

The Governor's wife circled her coffee cup with her hands, warming them briefly. From the corner of his eye, the Senate Majority Leader observed the gesture and wondered how her fingers would feel against his cheek. He thought about walking around the State Capitol at night in the snow with the Governor's wife. He would offer her his gloves, and when she refused them, he would pull her hands into his overcoat pockets. Then she wouldn't be the Governor's wife anymore.

"*Now, I don't think I'm an alarmist . . . and I hope I am not a pessimist . . . but I must tell the people of this great State that I am very deeply concerned. For we see all around us the—.*"

She watched her husband with studied absorption, her eyes solemn, her lips slightly parted. She noticed, once again, that he was looking especially well this evening. Klieg lights: they were already collecting footage for the next campaign . . . ten- and twenty- and thirty-second daubs of her husband, from which they would fashion pointillist portraits of him for mass viewing. The klieg lights shone on his head, making a halo of his near-perfect hair. His face was suffused with the rich coloration of health, the clarity of intelligence. The Governor's wife watched him, her expresion almost rapt. She could feel the intensity of the crowd's assent in the air and in the marrow of her bones. He still amazed her.

In the back of the hall, the Governor's aides stood in a restless cluster by the door. The press secretary held a stop-watch in one hand, a drink in the other.

"The old man's really on tonight," the executive assistant muttered from one side of his mouth.

"You think everybody can hear all right?"

"We can, can't we?"

"Yeah . . . ."

"Damn, that's a great dress!" The Governor's personal secretary sighed. The two men looked at her as if she had mouthed an obscenity, and she grinned at them sourly. "I've heard the speech before," she said.

"*And so I come before you tonight . . . not jubilant in victory . . . not swollen with success . . . but not weighed down, either, by the responsibility with which you have entrusted me . . . . I am full of optimism, my friends . . . inspired by your—.*"

Really knows how to reach in and pull it out of them, the Senate Majority Leader thought. He wasn't jealous, only eager to learn. Watching the subtle gestures of the Governor's hands, he denied himself a glance at the small, attentive woman above whose head the Governor addressed his following.

"*I was telling my wife on our way down here this evening . . . .*"

Under the table her chilled fingers probed the invisible repair in her dress, pressing the seam as if it were a wound, deliberately seeking to confirm its existence. Though she realized her husband was talking about her, the substance made little difference. Nothing he said would ever be quite like new again. But he needed her. Her hand stopped moving across her mended lap and lay still.

"*And I am going to tell you, my friends, exactly what I told her, for this is what I truly—.*"

PUBLIC APPEARANCES

The lady in the purple dress looked longingly at the plate of pastries in the center of the table. No one had even touched them, the plate was too far to reach without standing up. They always put the best things in the middle, she thought, where you couldn't get your hands on them.

"He's getting ready to wind 'er up," the press secretary murmured, looking approvingly at the stopwatch. "Right on schedule."

That dress is no color at all, the Lieutenant Governor's wife thought. Cost a fortune, though. When her day came, hers and Bernie's, she'd wear red. Red would stand out in a crowd.

"*And I promise you* . . . ."

Lost, the Senate Majority Leader thought. She looks absolutely lost. His hands rested, helpless, on the edge of the table.

Gathering speed and scattering power like sparks, the Governor raised his hands and his voice together, sending them out to meet the crowd more than halfway. Flashbulbs popped in a vehement, almost steady string of explosions. The Governor's wife saw red, a shower of red blotting out the room and the ocean of hands and mouths. She was lost.

"*And I promise you* . . . ."

She swallowed hard, a foretaste of disaster on her tongue. It always came at such moments: she would hear the crack of a single shot, see her husband fall. Red would bloom on his shirtfront, a bouquet of blood-roses clutched to his chest, pearl studs glistening among them like dewdrops. His eyes, full of promise still, would struggle to stay open, to find her. Wide and blue with the true believer's sudden disbelief, her husband's mortally wounded eyes. He needed her, beside him. But she wouldn't be able to find her way to him. She would be long lost. No help at all.

"*The day will come* . . . ."

The Governor's wife shut her eyes. Above her the familiar

voice, amplified, rose unharmed, stronger than ever. The hot white lights beat down on her face as she opened her eyes again and gazed up into the aura of promise surrounding her husband's near-perfect hair.

He possessed magical powers. She knew about magic. She understood it was that he was giving them, and why. They needed him. Their need was one of those things she had come to accept. And she understood that her premonition of mayhem was simply another of those false directions in which she constantly seemed to be getting lost. She steadied her sight, now, in her husband's direction.

"... *moving forward* ... *together* ... *toward tomorrow*."

Twelve hundred people—she no longer questioned the figure—jumped to their feet with one deafening roar, a sound that seemed to swell, threatening to burst the hall like a huge balloon. Beneath her, the platform bucked and swayed with the pounding.

The Governor bowed his head under the barrage of adulation, a half-smile on his face. As the ovation mounted, he remained perfectly still, almost as if he were resting. Then he turned to his left and held out a hand to his wife, pulling her in to join him inside the circle of blinding light.

As she was captured in a dozen camera lenses, the Governor's wife felt something leave her, something she realized she simply could not hold onto anymore. Magic ... she could no longer keep a place for it. It was, like mayhem, a belief she could no longer afford to indulge.

As the band struck up "Goodnight, Ladies," and the cameras clicked, the Governor's wife was presented with a spray of deep red roses. Carefully, she held the flowers so that they concealed the flaw in her dress.

While the photographers were still shooting, the Governor leaned toward his wife, bringing his lips close to her cheek.

"How was I, do you think?" he whispered.

"Perfect," she said. "Just perfect."

WILD MEN OF BORNEO

My father, seventy-nine, squats in a square of morning light. His hands, removing snails from a jade plant, look naked, shamed in the glare of the California sun. These hands never meant to live so long, their fingers pared down to nothing. Yet they move rapidly, plucking the snails with surgical steadiness. The family fortune: my father's hands.
"You're looking good, Pa," I say.
He doesn't look up from the cluster of deep green leaves, cushy as the pads of children's thumbs. "So you said. Last night."
He picked me up at the airport himself, crawling through Los Angeles at rush hour, locked behind tinted windows in the Buick's conditioned air. He was an hour early for my arrival. I, his son, didn't take my eyes off my watch during landing. The flight was already twenty minutes late as we started our descent: I was keeping the old man waiting. Even in retirement, he remains a surgeon. I imagined him in the airport's sordid men's room, scrubbing up, watching the clock.
"Guess the climate agrees with you," I say. Lame: the physician's son.
He looks up. "*I* agree with *it*," he tells me smoothly. "Why fight it?"
My father turns from me and raises his eyes to the piercingly clear sky. The light is like that in a hospital amphitheater, uncomplaisant and antiseptic. He smiles grimly, a man perfectly accustomed to prolonging life beyond the point of diminishing marginal returns.

My father and I have much in common. We lack for nothing but wives. We are both in positions to see to our own comforts. We admire, on strictly-timed visits, one another's amenities, for we are men who appreciate comfortable lives. Born to a tradition of tact, we delete references to the wives who abandoned us. My father managed to keep his for thirty-three years. I could hold onto mine for only five.

We speak of "my mother," of course. But somehow, in death, she has divided like an amoeba. "My mother" is another woman, not my father's wife. When she died of cancer of the colon, my father, saviour of lives, could not help but take it as a personal affront. Her death humiliated him. Now when he speaks of "your mother," his tones of sorrow are tokens of affection for me. His wife is another case entirely, a strictly forbidden topic, a buried mistake.

My father told me a year or so ago of a predatory, gabby widow he met at a cocktail party. She plied him with questions about his past and prospects. "What about your late wife?" she said.

"My wife," my father told her, "has never been late."

Now I do not believe my father actually said this. He is a helplessly courteous man. But he *wanted* to say it, which is more to the point. I suspect him of secretly worshipping a recollection of a dim creature who was always on time. However, he does not speak of her, nor have her in mind, when he says to me, "your mother."

He knows I am about to leave him. He understands that I have come to California to tell him so. My last visit is not long enough past to justify this one. Besides, it is April, and my usual journeys are dictated by the fiscal year. My father knows I have come to take my leave.

He will not deign to inquire. He will not permit me to wedge the announcement easily into our conversation if he can help it. But he is waiting for me to hammer it home, I can tell.

He takes me out to lunch. We sit at a chrome and oak table, separated from Balboa Bay by a wall of amber glass. My father eats a club sandwich, impressing me still with his capable hands, his own teeth. He wears his gardening clothes—a yellow porkpie hat, plaid pants, a red cardigan. I admire the jauntiness he has acquired in retirement, a bold adaptation to this unnatural habitat. Perhaps he has cultivated brazen visibility as a means of survival. Now that he can no longer play golf, he seems to take pains to look as if he does.

"Your mother loved it here," he says.

"The Yacht Club?"

"California. She said it made her think the world wasn't so old, after all."

I smile.

"She couldn't get over the fruits and vegetables in winter. I thought avocadoes and kiwi fruit would start sprouting from my ears. And she'd bring the damnedest-looking squash home from the Safeway . . . ."

I see my opening. "You miss her, Pa," I say.

My father sets the mangled triangle of his sandwich firmly on the edge of his plate. When he looks at me, his light gray eyes are steely. I imagine this is the expression he used to buck up patients who must be made to accept bad news. "Your mother had a great deal of . . . zest," he says.

He is not about to brook a second opinion.

The fact is, my mother was frail. In her opinions, more than her person. She fell in love with my father the year she lost her own. I, by the time I was twelve, could convince her of anything, provided my father left me to my own devices. My mother, my father's wife, was a woman weakened by respect for men. She laid her fragile doubts to rest in a warm cradle of affection and regard, and bridled her own enthusiasms. My father and I could come and go as we pleased. She always waited for us.

Sometimes my mother cried in the afternoons. But she always swore she didn't. The days must have been long for her. Waiting. Some days I would come home late from school to find her sitting in the darkened living room, on the edge of the piano bench, at the bass end of the keyboard. There would be no sheet music in sight, and my mother never could play from memory. I would switch on the old brass floor lamp, and the silk shade would cast a false golden glow over her face, her auburn hair, her narrow shoulders.

"You're home," she'd say, as if I'd done something miraculous. The lids of her eyes would be rosy and swollen.

At a certain age, I was not too cautious to ask if she'd been crying. She always denied it with a girlish laugh. In time, perhaps to forestall my indelicate question, she moved from the piano bench to the crewel-work wingback chair beside the fireplace. She would hold a book in her lap, and listen for the door to open so she could switch on a lamp before I reached the room.

"Have you been crying, Mom?"

"A sad book, lovey. I'm a silly old sob-sister." I permitted her laugh to convince me. She became an admirer of Anne Morrow Lindbergh and other brave lady-writers who had outlived their children.

I never told my father that his wife, my mother, wept behind his back. I expected him to know it, just as she expected me to guard her secret. My father was a brilliant doctor, with a gift for diagnostics. At the very least, he should have seen the days were bound to be long for her.

Two and a half years ago, after my mother's funeral, I did not look at her husband to see if he cried when her cushioned, polished casket was cradled in the sandy California ground. I was afraid for a moment I might hate him either way, despise his strength or his weakness. I edged closer to him and kept my eyes on my ex-wife, Linda, who stood with the minor mourners on the opposite side of the grave. Linda and my mother had been very fond of each other. I distracted myself from my father by wondering if my wife had ever been reduced to tears by the unbearable weight of a long afternoon.

Although they had courted me for several years, I accepted a position with the World Bank only after my father and I had lost our wives. I could not leave my whereabouts to chance, knowing women waited for me. Linda might have come along wherever I went, of course, and we had no children. But each time I considered the prospect of a foreign post, there arose a pathetic picture of my wife languishing in a hammock in Karachi or Calcutta with the sun still high in the sky. I heard her soft, desperate voice struggling to confide in some Swahili-speaking houseboy, or haggling over a piece of stringy meat at a stall in the Casbah. I toyed with such scraps of imagination until I froze fast to them, like a child's tongue stuck to a metal fencepost in winter. I tore myself away from exotic ambitions, claimed the World Bank was a poor risk: some parts of the world are not fit to be seen by a man with dependents.

I neglected, however, to extrapolate my theories to Maclean, Virginia. I hastened to my office at the Brookings Institution each morning and never paused to ask how my wife spent her days. She mistook my conscientiousness for passion, my confidence for disregard. When she left me, I found her, for the first time, stunning. Not long ago she married a linguist from Georgetown and moved to Peru without batting an eye. Like my mother, Linda was sadly underestimated.

When the World Bank tendered what I felt would be its final offer, I discussed it with my father. I could not calculate the precise effect my whereabouts might have on him.

"They could send me to some pretty out-of-the-way places," I said.

"You're young," he told me, as if that answered everything.
"For two- or three-year hitches," I said.
"It's your decision, son."
"But what about you?"
He gazed past my shoulder toward an oil portrait of my mother, the oddly incongruous gift his colleagues had commissioned to mark his retirement from the staff of Sloan-Kettering. "I always wanted to see Borneo when I was a boy," he said.
"Borneo. Imagine."
"Why Borneo?"
"'The Wild Men of Borneo.' In those days, all the circuses and carnivals had them." He seemed to study me speculatively for a moment, taking my measure. "Before your time," he said.

I waited for him to continue, but he didn't. "I guess that settles it, then," I said foolishly.

My father nodded, his expression solemn and innocent, sealing a bargain without logic. The lack of irony in his eyes aged him in mine.

That was two years ago. I have yet to see Borneo, but I have traveled to South America, Africa, the Far East. I have explored the economic ruins of world powers, the fiscal jungles of developing nations. I have kept a sharp eye on deficits, gross national products, and per capita incomes while governments toppled. At the World Bank, as at Brookings, I have earned a reputation as a "troubleshooter," a cool correspondent of currency wars. I, however, prefer to regard myself as merely a chip off the old block—a man with a gift for diagnostics.

Now I am to be rewarded for the slim margin of error in my second guesses: Tokyo. The assignment is something of a plum. I have been promised a host of benefits: administrative autonomy, car with driver, the opportunity to sway world markets.

My flight departs from Dulles one week from tomorrow. I have come to take leave of my father. He knows, without being told. He waits through the long afternoon.
"What time is your plane on Sunday?" It is Friday.
"Early. Seven-thirty."
He nods. "No traffic problems, then."
"Why don't I just get a limousine?"
I am dismissed with a gesture, a wave of his still-competent hand. "How about some Mexican food tonight?" he says. "There's this place Nixon loved in San Juan Capistrano . . . ."
I give the old man credit: he has managed to work the evils of politics and the perils of foreign travel into a single proposition. He is a master of the suggestive remark.
"Sure. I could go for some chiles rellenos."
"And margaritas. We'll make a night of it."
He is waiting.
"Pa—."
"So, where's it going to be?"
"The place in San Juan Capistrano sounds fine," I say.
His laugh is brutally abbreviated, like the bark of a dog with a choke-chain clutching its throat. I remember him telling me once, long ago, "The first incision's always the hardest to make . . . but it shouldn't be. That's rarely the one a patient dies from."
"Tokyo, Pa. Next week."
"For how long?"
My fingers curl, tighten, as if I am holding a scalpel. I relax them, force my own hand to hold firm. "For a couple of years, anyway."
"Tokyo . . . sounds like you're moving up pretty fast, boy."

I shrug. It wouldn't do, now, to tell him about the living allowance, influence on exchange rates, a waiting driver, the balance of trade.

"Tokyo." He shakes his head. "Not exactly Borneo, is it?"

The restaurant is crowded. Even with a reservation, we have to wait twenty minutes for a table. My father and I, two independent men, stand side by side at the blue and white tiled bar, drinking margaritas. A swag of plastic peppers festoons a mirrored arch, the bartender's proscenium. Absurdly young and beautiful, he performs with the staccato precision of a picador among the lustrous glasses and whirring chrome machines.

The old man plays host, drawing me out about world gold prices, the Federal Reserve. He has put on a navy blue blazer, a vague nautical insignia on its breast pocket. His handkerchief is paisley silk. Coarse salt glimmers at the corners of his mouth.

I catch myself stumbling, losing the strength of my convictions under my father's merciless charm. Then there is the inevitable lull. He lets me off the hook.

"Sorry about the wait, son."

"Friday nights," I say.

"Funny . . . time always seems so much longer when you're waiting for something." He sets his thick-lipped greenish glass on the bar and spreads his hands on either side of it. He stares in mild astonishment at how they betray him. "I'm beginning to understand what your mother . . . what Claire . . . meant."

Speechless, I touch my father's sleeve.

"She'd use that expression, 'time hangs heavy on your hands.' I never understood her."

Beneath my fingers, my father's bent elbow twitches, once, as if he is trying to shake me off. "She was always waiting for something, your mother."

"We all are, Pa."

"I suppose so."

In the next room, a mariachi band is playing "Vaya con Dios."

"Don't get me wrong," my father says, "but I wish sometimes you'd been a girl."

Indescribable pain fills my chest, suffocating me. My father observes, making a swift, sure diagnosis.

"It just might be easier, son."

"How?"

"If you were a daughter, maybe I could ask you not to go."

"What if I went anyway?"

My father looks away, through the archway into the crowded, noisy dining room. He tilts his head to one side, seems to be listening to the music, inhaling the over-spiced air. There is a twisted smile on his salty lips.

"Tonight I'd dance with you," he says.

A waitress in an embroidered blouse approaches us. There is a string of veined turquoise beads around her neck. She has the coarse-grained, unfinished look of a primitive madonna. "Your table is ready, sir." She addresses me, not my father.

My old man lifts his glass. "To Tokyo," he says.

"To Borneo," I correct him, gently touching my glass to his.

He takes my arm and allows me to lead him into the next room.

ONE HUNDRED YEARS OF SOLICITUDE: THE MEDITATIONS OF URSULSA

ONE HUNDRED YEARS OF SOLICITUDE

They dress me like a doll. A baby doll. They entwine mango leaves in the sparse groves of my hair, twisting and giggling and denting my skin and bones with their nails, their teeth. Baby teeth. They rock me, when I wish only for the stillness, the safe motionless vacuum which is what a home should be. But *mi casa* is overrun with children. Red ants. Cockroaches. The edges of the jungle impinge on us here, and I can do nothing. I, a hostage, offered to the children like a sugar tit, to keep them happy.

Ah, and they *are* happy. Pleased with me. They wind me in the table linens of my finicky daughter-in-law, the one without mercy. The Beauty has gone to meet the clouds more than halfway, and I am left to the carpenter ants, the ceaseless drip of remembered rains, the tablecloth shroud. I am left to the children.

Whose children are they? No children of mine. The lineage lengthens until I can no longer tell where they came in. Though it pains me to say so, my son must take some of the blame for this smudging of the line. My son the hero—he dabbled in arts he didnt' understand: war, alchemy, compromise. And paternity: he scattered children behind him like breadcrumbs, to find his way back, perhaps. But he didn't make it. And now they are pecking my eyes out, these bright and flighty little pests with sharp beaks. Children: the price of my son the hero's squandered breadcrumbs.

But is that right? Not fair . . . but *right*, true, correct? Possibly not. (The century carries more weight than memory can bear, and the mango leaves throw shadows on my eyes.) It is possibly wrong to take to task the memory of my son the hero for these ants, these birds, this army of children. He sired a ragtag regiment of sons, it is true. I remember their names, all seventeen of them. But they did not set this whiplash of progeny in motion. How could they, those ash-marked doomsboys with their fatalistic mothers and their fatal flaws? I remember a time when everyday was Ash Wednesday in Macondo: the priest's chocolate-dark lips began the next Dies Irae before finishing the first. My son left bodies behind him, not children.

It goes hard with me now, at the hands of the children. I sometimes think I wasn't cut out to be a matriarch. But that is the kind of thing you never know until you try. If they speak of me in the next hundred years or so, I hope they will say this:

> She tried.

But how can I expect it? On what can hope rest? The children do not speak. They fly. They chirp and crow. They peck at my bones. But words—those will not live after me. Speech is one of the gypsy tricks that failed. Even my husband, the would-be sorcerer, didn't know what to do with them. Words—they killed my sons and spoiled my daughter's beauty. There will be no one to speak of my life. Perhaps it is better this way. Still, I wish there would be someone to mourn me with a simple sentence:

> She tried.

Yes, hard it goes, hard and deep as the petrified roots of my husband. They say he no longer adorns my garden, but I disregard this and keep wondering: how does he fare in this heavy rainfall? I suspect it goes hard with him, too. Antiquity is no easy business, whether you are a tree or a doll. But then nothing is easy. Almost nothing. The only facile thing I ever did in my life was making the little candy animals. Green rabbits, tangerine monkeys, cats the color of passion fruit . . . so simple and apparently harmless. And look what happened—one uncomplicated task, and I put the whole village to sleep. Set my husband to a frenzy of labeling he never quite recovered from. Stole my people's collective memory . . . I might have been shot, that's where easy gets you.

ONE HUNDRED YEARS OF SOLICITUDE

I did hide the gold, of course. That was easy, too. But I had the help of a saint: Joseph, the childless father, patron of the ambiguous. My devotion to him was misdirected, I later learned. I do not list the safekeeping of someone else's coins among my personal achievements.

So, antiquity falls hard. Harder than revolution or betrothal or remembering the names of things and their uses. But the helplessness of age is preferable to ruinous, ageless powers: magnets, for instance. Or ice. Melquiades the homewrecker must have foreseen this. Antiquity has its charms, its prizes. There is a system of reparations: for everything you forget, there is something you understand.

I try to explain this to the children who, somewhere along the line, are mine.

They twitter and poke their little talons into my useless eyes and tie a babushka over my leafy hair. They call me *Mamacita*, interrogating me about buried treasure and lying to me about who, and whose, they are.

I have a million stories—average compensation, no more, for the time I've put in. A hundred years is no record, believe me, not in this part of the world. A century, I ask myself, and what have I got to show for it? The tapestries are gone, the lamps shattered, the pianola made to my order by that beautiful boy is as dry of music as a coconut fallen outside its tree's shade. I know, now, no Pope will ever come of Macondo. The jungle, the rains, and the ants have turned my village into a pagan burial ground. My home remains a bone of contention among warring appetites. Only one issue is settled: *mi casa* is no longer mine. So what have I saved for retirement? What is the pension for one hundred years' labor?

I have a million stories.

Naturally, everyone wants to hear about my son the hero, the favorite among those inclined to worship or ridicule. Disappointment attended him: too much the fool for some, not enough for others. He was loved by legions, but I alone understood him, only I. Dangling the last of the golden fishes like a hypnotist's timepiece, I tell how he suffered visions as a boy. This satisfies everyone. Otherwise, I guard the secrets of my son the hero, sparing history the account of his decline. I play my part: long-lost mother tongue of Macondo.

I could be no more frank or generous where the other boy is concerned, even if anybody asked. My son the squatter, feeding his wife's hunger with stolen soil. Big plans . . . *muy grande* . . . almost got away with them, too. And when he didn't . . . well, at least another thousand stories there. I read his fate years before, in the foreign maps on his hide, his taunting manliness. He did not consult me in his choice of a bride, but when he died a door away from her, it was to me his blood came scuttling. To *Mamacita*. I rinsed him from the linoleum borders of *mi casa*, allowing my firstborn to remain a mystery, his death an unholy miracle.

Then there was the third child, the girl-child. Her name hinted at the forgotten word (its uses also forgotten) for love. Unfortunately, my one true daughter was a black widow spider. I tried to do what I could for her. I was not successful. Now, when the children leave me to myself, I am kept busy . . . erasing the countless dark, crabbed stories of my spider girl. If any are left at the end, I shall take them to the grave with me. Or to the urn—wherever they dispose of me when they tire of playing pick-up-sticks with my bones.

No, I am not one of those women who would stultify the universe with her children's exploits. I keep my stories where they do the least harm: in my head. And I refuse, as well, to be one of those widows (if indeed I *am* a widow—I am unconvinced, as I feel the branches and roots snaking through the soil below the rotting house even now) . . . I firmly decline the pathetic prerogatives of the garrulous widow who would preach to the young from the edge of her husband's grave. I'll say only this: my husband was a dreamer. I adored that in him, even as I despised his dreams. He required a very firm hand. It was a struggle: *mano a mano, mano a boca.* And I deserve some credit, for even after he went completely mad, flailing at the wall of the house, flinging down tiles from the roof over my head, I never kept secrets from him. Children today do not understand that this—the obliteration of secrets—is the very cornerstone of marriage. And how would the ancient and experienced (such as myself) instruct them? It is difficult to hand down wisdom, or anything at all, what with the ants carrying the house away and the words, by oversight unlabeled when memory began to slip, now utterly forgotten by all but a baby doll in a babushka.

No, there will never be stories about my husband embroidered in the parlors of strangers or distant kin. I knew that I had, in a sense, won, when they told me he was putting down roots out there, right in sight of my bedroom window. But I don't go bragging about it. When the surrealist botanists of other countries come begging ('How often was he watered . . . pruned?' 'Did you save a few leaves, that we might study him?') I press my lips together, pretending my ears are as useless as these gauzy eyes. Marriage is unspeakably private. Stories should not be told of it.

Perhaps it is simply because I am a woman that I find the stories of the women in my family more fascinating than the men's. Or possibly the women, coming from outside my own womb (other than the spider, whom I mean to erase) seem more exotic to me. The girls my boys brought home . . . the girls their boys stashed under my eaves: shiny, frail, tough, magical, musky creatures that boys wrap up and carry home like trophies, fire at each other like pistols. The women of the family, acquired, account for most of the million stories allotted to me for my longevity.

Then, too, the stories of women tend to be cautionary, and lend themselves more readily to my manner of telling. With women's stories, I have an edge of insight, a center of empathy.

So if I were to begin spinning yarns . . . if the wicked children would stop bouncing and decorating my remains . . . I might commence in this vicinity:

With the moonstruck orphan who rocked and sucked and tried to eat the earth as she waited for my son, that paisley creature of the deep, to surface, to flood her ravenous cavity. For her I learned the secret remedy of oranges and rhubarb (I, the realist with unmasked contempt for secret remedies, my opposition to quick fixes a matter of record).

Warming up as I went along, I might possibly reveal how this girl's voracious dirt-hunger shamed the woman (*this* woman) who would have been her mother, who yearned to stuff that little belly and all the world with bread and cake and jewel-hued barley sugar beasts. And how the wild refusal of the starving sprite with grass stuck between her teeth to let me succor her made me love her all the more, until I thought the love might kill me more quickly than the hard lumps of Macondo ground could kill her. Yes. I might even confess (to a *simpatico* audience) that this child was, with her muddy gums and fierce digging, more my own child than my own children were . . . .

Groping through the family closets for a shred of loveliness, I should then recall the girl of accomplished passions whose daring filled the house with yellow butterflies. My face brushed by swarms of wings, I was reminded what I myself once meant to be. It was too late. Paralysis, banishment . . . they planted her infant in the bulrushes, and I received him, pretending to swallow one more virgin birth. A matriarch must be hospitable to myth, regardless of its origin.

ONE HUNDRED YEARS OF SOLICITUDE

Where next? My confidence expanding like a brood hen's feathers, puffed and iridescent with maternal pride, I would disclose the glittering gem in my crown of aloe and cactus thorns: the childbride I loved better than my son the hero and all his ash-strewn sons and fine filagree and pomp and victories. I would tell how she came to me (not to her own mother, as the conventional version has it), clapping her baby hands with delight at the first smear of womanhood, warm and rich as the priest's sacrificial chocolate. If I lived in an age when pictures could still be painted with words, I would depict this: how the baby-woman embraced me and asked me to tell her a wife's secrets and I told them, every one, without blushing and she understood as no one in my own household ever understood me before or since.

This almost-angel followed my son the hero to my doorway, toting dolls and pointless, complicated games in veneered boxes, kite string and a flute and a collection of pressed flowers, petite white boots and a large yellow ball that resembled the mid-morning sun. I built shelves for her childhood hoard with my own hands, and changed the linen on the bridal bed every single day for as long as she stayed in my house. (My son assumed, like any man, that my solicitude had to do with his heroics, his piddling virility. He never caught on that only his winning me this child of my later years arranged his hero's welcome in my heart, negotiated my settlement with him.)

I cherished this new daughter like a holy relic, cleaned all my proud rooms cleaner than they had ever been so that she could decorate them with her innocence. I began to fashion the candy animals again, and never had they been so brilliantly colored, so exquisitely detailed and lifelike, so tasty . . . I forgot what happens to all one should remember when sleep is thrown to the dogs of lemon sugar, the guava-flavored birds. I gave the childbride free run in *mi casa* and soul, and we were happier than women were meant to be in Macondo. The angelvoices were coming closer: I heard, but didn't listen. I neglected to label them as household hazards, letting absentmindedness get the better of me again.

And then one day, two frail and flighty generations later, among the flapping sheets, clean and wet and windfilled like sails I meant to launch on the sea I once discovered (when my husband was otherwise engaged), the angels landed at last. Cherubim, seraphim: they took Beauty, queen of the bloody carnival, to a place where sainthood could be pursued without the deaths and distractions of men . . . .

These days I worship at an altar in my sitting room, facing an imperfect likeness behind a vigil light that perpetually wants to go out (would I allow it). The atmosphere is heavenly with dust. A saintly shroud has been woven by tent caterpillars . . . .

Pobrecitas, my darlings . . . I don't know which of you is most missed in *mi casa,* Innocence or Beauty. I mourn, while in another room, the decimation of the household linens is eulogized.

By all rights, this is where the stories should stop. One of my grandsons (not exactly legitimate and removed by many greats), the one who lives in books in the back of the house, says stories should end precisely upon the peak of intensity. (He speaks of this as a geographical location he has passed many times.) I believe he does know something of this, for our story nearly stops with him. So he is probably right. But I also know myself: the kind of woman who, were she to begin unraveling the family history, would not know when to quit. Where would we be then?

Should I tell of the household whore who battered her way up my back stoop on rippling thighs to usurp my place as

ONE HUNDRED YEARS OF SOLICITUDE

grandmother? She seduced both my sons in turn, and if that weren't enough, she later bore my grandson's child. (He, her son, was a hawker of decrees, daguerreotypes, and dressy uniforms. What good could come of such a mother?) Still, the slattern was my closest friend for many years. She saw beyond the present. We understood one another.

And if I could speak of someone so unspeakable, then I could probably bring myself to tell also of the princess-in-exile claiming sanctuary in *mi casa* with her golden pisspot . . . the one who weakened the foundation, and my hold on it, more surely than the carpenter ants with their age-old penchant for demolition and clearance . . . .

Then before I knew it, heated with my listeners' rapt attention, no doubt I'd be spilling the beans about the great-great-granddaughter (I think that's where she came in) who skipped to Belgium. She slipped from her dark-veiled duenas somewhere among the Flemish guildhalls, I believe, leaving a trail of stout brogans and middy blouses. She would reappear in Macondo eventually (they all do) with vile habits, garish gowns, and a mustachioed and winged husband older and better than she deserved . . . but how would I know about that, I who had nothing to do with the gypsies?

You see the danger of having a rapt audience: one gets lured in, egged on, to subjects one really knows nothing about.

The children drag me to the old stone tub now. They are about to give me my daily dip among the scorpions. Bird droppings encrust the rim of the basin, once worn smooth with my scrubbing. I do not know if it is a blessing or a curse that they neglect, as always, to remove my clothes before they drop me into the sordid water. Surely I am not eager to expose more of my flesh to them. They take enough liberties with me as it is, pronounce me dead. But my long, dark garments, waterlogged, grow heavy as boulders. They set me out in the sun to dry, sometimes forgetting about me for days. The birds light in the nest the bird-like children have made of my hair, pluck parts of me for their summer homes.

I sit behind the house and pray for good weather, warm sun and an hospitable breeze. I stare at the great old trees I allowed to remain when I thought shade a desirable thing, a protection of sorts . . . I study the thick, gnarled trunks and try to recognize the father of my children among them. They all look familiar, of course . . . but I don't have the feeling I've been intimate with any of them.

The babushka is slipping down my forehead. Already it covers my brows. Concealed, the mango leaves decay. Why should I mind? My eyes are not what they used to be . . . let the children cover them and have their fun with me. Dress me like a baby doll. I don't have the stamina to tangle with insects anymore . . . let us share the territory. If *mi casa* lasts another generation, it will be only for those pigtailed descendants I've been expecting all along. A few years ago, I might have straightened everything out by plunging into the candy animal business again. Or by shaking my husband the tree loose from his dream-roots for a time. In desperation, I might even have called my son the hero home from battle for the height of the growing season.

I hear the children splashing in the tub themselves now. I wonder if they have disrobed? They are no more modest than the birds. Or Beauty. The frayed edge of the babushka rests on the bridge of my nose: I see nothing. But I can feel something warm spreading across my lap. Perhaps the sun is finally coming out. It is not altogether unpleasant to sit here . . . until the children need their baby doll again. (I am, even now, a mother: I wish to be useful.) It would do no good to be telling tales now, anyway . . . even if the words could clarify them-

ONE HUNDRED YEARS OF SOLICITUDE

selves. I swear I can hear the carpenter ants sawing off pieces of my home . . . swallowing chunks of the leftovers of Macondo.

There is not a thing I can do to hold things together anymore. I shall just sit here quietly, the warmth like a damp-diapered infant on my lap, and try to remember what it was like to remember . . . .

Perhaps if I remain perfectly still . . . perhaps if the children forget about me for a day or two . . . perhaps the details will return to rearrange themselves. It would be worth a hundred years, if only I could see it once more from behind these liquid eyes, cloudy as Pernod:

How the angels came down and trampled my fresh laundry in their eagerness to make away with the one true saint of my household . . . .

How radiant she looked as she rose above my head . . . .

How she hung there for a moment, as if she didn't care to leave me at all, floating bright and pure, with all that wet white linen flapping under her feet . . . .

If a priest remained in this God-forsaken village, if there were still beings who held with words, I would make my confession one of these days. In public or in private, without the slightest design on absolution, I would confess what the best of my million stories omits: how I prayed for the angels to take me. A wish . . . .

Wishes beget offspring, perhaps, but they do not provide for them. I had to stay, to work against many things: time, numbers, magnets, ice. In short:
I tried.

A strong wind seems to be coming up in the distance. I feel it in my bones: they are whistling. The rest, as they say, is history. And history is folly. Thank God this is something we don't understand for the first hundred years.

WALLS

WALLS

She began raising Cain about six weeks after the kid died.

The walls in our building are like cardboard, and having her in the apartment right next door was like having her in our own place. She called his name in this thin, whiny voice, the way kids will start up when they see they're not going to get their own way about something. It really got to me.

"Jesse . . . Jess-eee . . . ."

She'd sound like she was going to start crying any second. Only she didn't. Or if she did, we couldn't hear that part. I swear, though, it got so I could tell she was there—right behind the headboard of our bed, on the other side of the wall—even when she didn't make a sound.

At first we didn't realize it was the kid she was calling, because her old man was named Jesse, too. "Big Jesse" she called him when the kid was around—a huge, cheery guy with sort of a pigeon-toed walk and as much hair on his back as his front. Full reddish beard. He reminded me of a picture of Paul Bunyan in a book I had when I was a kid. Anyway, we'd see Big Jesse washing his car in the lot out back sometimes. He never wore a shirt if it was more than fifty degrees out. He had this hat that looked like it was made of Budweiser labels stitched together. He wore it pushed way back on his head.

The wife never started up until nearly an hour after Big Jesse had gone to work. There was always a lot of talk back and forth as he left for the plant in the morning—"Have a good day . . . I'll be a little late," that kind of thing. So we figured she must have known when he was gone. He told Ray, when they got talking once down by the trash chute, that he worked at the tool and die place out past the airport.

Ray and I were having troubles of our own. Not that anything is the same as losing a kid, of course. But things were getting shaky for us around that time, and we were doing a lot of late-night talking.

Ray drives an ambulance, and he was working the four-to-eleven shift at the hospital. I always make him a little something to eat, no matter what time he comes home. He loves Chef Boy-Ar-Dee ravioli, the meat ones. And Spaghettios. He'd eat and before you knew it we'd be off on these discussions—marathons. A lot of times we'd just be warming up around midnight.

Ray needs to talk awhile—"unwind," he says—before he can get to sleep. I could do without it, to tell the truth. I like to fall asleep telling myself happy stories, making up good things that might happen to me. Besides, I just can't understand how if people love each other, they can't see eye-to-eye—about what's important, at least. I hate arguing, especially when it gets mean. And it almost always does. I used to think my parents would wind up murdering each other with their mouths. But that was all over by the time I was seven or eight.

Ray and I got along just fine from the very first, though. Things had been great for a year and a half. So why all of a sudden he wanted to get married was beyond me. A wedding could throw everything out of whack. And for what? That's what I wanted to know.

"A year and a half . . . perfect," I said. "What are you after?"

"Going on *two* . . . what are you afraid of?"

"I'm not afraid. I just don't want to mess things up."

"See?" Ray shook his head. "You're afraid."

"Come on, honey. It's just I don't see the point. We're happy like it is. It's not as if we wanted kids or something."

Kids. I made no bones about that from the beginning. I wasn't about to start having kids at my age.

"Okay, okay." Ray turned away, looking confused, those big blue eyes of his kind of cloudy. "I wasn't talking about kids, was I? I'm talking about us."

"So what's getting married going to do for us? We're together, right?"

"It's different when you're married."

"Yeah, I remember." I knew it sounded sarcastic when I laughed. Ray and I were both married before. Both knew it wasn't any bed of roses.

He was looking out the window, up, at the sky. Chewing on the back of his thumb the way he does when he can't find the right words for what he's thinking.

"Ray, listen—we have the good part, the best part, of being married already. We *belong* to each other."

"People who are married belong to each other more," he said. "It's different."

How? I just couldn't see it. Getting married seems like a rope to me—if it doesn't strangle you, you trip on it. Why take the chance? We'd talk and talk and get no place fast. Finally we'd go to bed feeling kind of used-up and empty. Those nights, if we made love at all, it would seem like a continuation of the argument.

Even though we might have been in bed only a few hours, the noise Big Jesse made next door while he was getting ready for work didn't really bother us. We were used to it, and it was sort of sweet to hear this big moose singing in the shower. He knew every one of the Four Tops' big hits backwards and forwards. The funny thing was, he had the rhythm of a drill sergeant. Polish Soul, Ray called it. We'd get laughing, lying in our bed at six o'clock in the morning, hearing this big dumb voice singing, "Reach out (three-four), reach out (three-four), reach out to me-e (two-three-four) . . . ." Sometimes there'd be this thumping in four-quarter time, too. I think maybe he marched in the tub, when he really got into the music.

If Ray was in a good mood, and not still sore from our talking the night before, he'd take advantage of the interruption and move over to my side of the bed. The conversation in the next apartment put us in the mood to play around.

"Baloney okay today, hon?"

"Sure thing (three-four)."

By the time Big Jesse left for work at six-forty-five, Ray and I were usually good and ready to get back to sleep. We'd stay in bed until noon or so, resting up for the next marathon discussion. I was worn out, in more ways than one.

The name on their mailbox was Jankowski. We never got to know their kid, just saw him around. A cute little guy, maybe six or seven years old. He was husky, like his dad, and pigeon-toed, but he had the woman's coloring: blond hair, gray eyes, pale pink skin. Hardly any eyelashes. He reminded me, in a way, of a rabbit, one of those big white ones they sell at Easter time. It wasn't just his washed-out eyes. If the kid saw you watching him, he'd stand stock-still and sort of blink. With those thick haunches of his, he could have been a concrete lawn statue. Once he moved, though, really moved, he was the fastest thing you ever saw. He was always packed into these bulky sweaters, homemade-looking. And black sneakers that laced right up over the ankle. You could tell he was pretty strong for his age, too.

One time Ray was standing by the living room window and I went over to see what he was looking at. The little boy was roller skating on the sidewalk out front. What a sight. His arms and legs pushed like pistons. One-two-three-four. It was obvious where he got his sense of rhythm from. And this dead-serious expression on his meaty little face.

"Cute," I said.

Just then, the kid landed on his seat on the pavement, hard.

Ray grinned. "Little Polish ham," he said.

I thought he was just being mean, and I gave him a punch in the arm. But when I looked at his face, I realized it was only his smart mouth talking, as usual. He had that sort of soft expression he gets sometimes after we've made love—no arguments, no place to go.

WALLS

It was Rollie, the building super, who told us the kid was sick. Rollie's this old retired Irishman who thinks spreading bad news is part of his job. I wish he was half as good at the rest of it as he is at broadcasting other people's business. Anyway, one day Rollie came up to bring us some spray stuff that according to him is the only thing will kill roaches. (No matter how much I clean, we always have them around—Ray says they breed in the walls, that they're a thousand years old.)

I thanked Rollie for the spray, but he kept hanging around, like he had something on his mind. Finally, he worked his way around to telling us that the little Jankowski boy was in the hospital. Getting those treatments that make your hair fall out. That his chances looked pretty slim. I felt just sick, even though I hardly knew the people.

One day I passed her, the mother, in the hallway. Her name was Wanda, but I couldn't for the life of me remember it at the time. It was easy to see she hadn't been eating or sleeping right, even though she wasn't exactly what you'd call thin. And her hair was a mess, kind of wild-looking and growing in dark at the roots. Really bad split ends, the way those home permanents will do. I half-opened my mouth to say something to her, but she smiled tight and looked away, like she didn't want to talk. We both said "hi" and kept going. For some reason, afterwards I kept wishing I could have worked on her hair, fixed it up for her. Funny, the dumb things that will cross your mind.

About a month later, when Rollie told us the kid was on his way out, I still hadn't come up with anything I could say or do. I thought about baking a cake or something, leaving it by their door. Two or three more days and Ray saw in the paper that the kid had died. There was a picture of him, wearing a little bow tie. A real heartbreaker.

It's strange, and sort of terrible, how you can practically live with somebody, nothing but a flimsy piece of beaver-board and some pipe and wire between you, and not have the slightest idea what's going on with them. Except for Rollie and the newspaper, Ray and I wouldn't have known. We'd hardly seen the kid in the first place, or even heard him. We probably wouldn't have noticed how the old man's singing died down. Sure, things were pretty quiet over there, but they might have gone on vacation. Come down with the flu. We wouldn't have thought a thing about it, I bet.

"We ought to do something," I told Ray, when he showed me the obit.

"What can you do?" He shrugged and looked at the sidewalk outside, but I could tell he felt like crying. The corners of his mouth moved like they couldn't decide whether to go up or down.

"It says, 'contributions to Saint Jude's Children's Hospital in lieu of flowers,'" I said.

Ray made this funny little sound of disgust, like dry spit. "Flowers."

"We could send a check. To the hospital."

"Yeah. Okay."

But the newspaper didn't give the address, and I couldn't remember where the place was, even though I've seen Danny Thomas talking about it on television a hundred times. After awhile, I guess we just forgot.

The first time I saw Jesse's mother after the funeral—we ran into each other in the laundry room—I made it a point not to look away, to make my smile real serious. She stared at me for a second, nodded, then slammed the door of a dryer and left fast. I felt like a jerk for not saying something, but I hoped she knew . . . I mean, what can you say, really?

Eventually the noises next door started getting back to normal. Big Jesse even sang in the shower sometimes, but he never really sounded the same.

Maybe I would have paid more attention if the trouble hadn't heated up between Ray and me. Not that paying attention would have changed anything. Anyhow, we had enough problems without looking to borrow some from the neighbors.

When Ray brought up the marriage idea in the first place, he said it was "just something he wanted to run by me." When I put him off, though, he started getting stubborn, like his mind was made up. And he acted like I'd done something bad to him.

"Honey," I said, "this is such a dumb thing to be fighting about."

"It's not dumb. It's a question of if we love each other enough."

"Right. Fighting over how much we love each other—it's dumb." I reached over and tried to rub his neck, thinking I could calm him down, but he pulled away.

"Listen, Ray, I *love* you." I sounded like I was begging for a favor.

Ray gave me a dirty look. "You don't understand anything," he said.

I remembered how he'd told me the same thing about his wife once. That was when I first met him, two years ago March, in the Dark Alley, that cocktail lounge at the Ten Pin. I was there with a couple of girls from work. Ray was by himself, having a few beers after getting off at the hospital. He and Renee, one of the girls I was with, knew each other somehow. Ray came over and sat in our booth, and I could tell he noticed me. I had just frosted my hair and cut it in one of those short shags. I was almost twenty-nine, but short hair makes me look younger. Also, I take good care of my skin.

Renee and them took off about one o'clock, but I was still in the booth with Ray at two-thirty when the place closed. He drove me home. That was when he told me about his wife. He'd just gotten his divorce the week before, and he was on top of the world.

"I can't believe I'm out of it," he said. "Finally."

"Pretty bad, huh?"

"You ever been married?"

I looked out my side of the car and saw a drunk leaning against a Yield sign at the corner of Forest and Cermak. Behind him, every single window in the Grandview Apartments was dark. I wondered what it was like to live in a place that had an elevator, chairs in the lobby. Where you had to press a buzzer and have one answer you back before you could get past your own front door.

"In high school," I said.

Ray laughed. "High school shouldn't count."

"I'm with you there."

"I liked being married, though. Just not to her."

"She must have been pretty terrible."

"Terrible? Nah. She just didn't understand anything. That was all." He was watching me out of the corner of his eye while he drove. "I'm not down on being married, though."

I never heard a guy say anything like that before. It seemed sweet and sad to me, like a little kid who pretends not to know the end of a story he's heard a million times, so you'll read it to him again.

We pulled up at a stoplight, and Ray looked right at me for a minute. "She just didn't understand things," he said in a sad voice. "We couldn't talk."

When I didn't say anything, he drove through the intersection. The light hadn't changed yet.

"You ran a red light," I said.

He shrugged. "Nothing to stop for."

"There was too."

"Yeah—what?"

"The light," I said.

Ray looked at me sidewise, speeding up the car. "I think I'm just what you need," he said.

He was right. He was good for me. In a way, I felt like I had a chance to start life over again, to get it right this time. As if high school really didn't count. Ray made me feel like a winner. But now he was making me feel like two cents. Talking about me the way he used to talk about his wife. It hurt plenty.

Me being out of work wasn't helping matters, either. Crowning Glory, the beauty salon where I'd been for almost three years, had closed, another down-city small business wiped out by the big mall near the Interstate. I'd been looking for a new place for a couple months, but no luck. I just kept hoping somebody in the business would elope or get knocked-up. I was going stir-crazy. And Ray was real good about it, never complained, but the money situation was tight.

I thought it would help when Ray was taken off the four-to-eleven shift and put on seven-to-four. His having to get up early would cut down the midnight marathons. Driving an ambulance, like Ray always says, is nothing you'd want to do with your eyes half-open. You've got to be on your toes every second.

His new schedule gave us a chance to go out some, too. We could do things we hadn't been able to do for a long time. Go bowling and shopping together. Meet other couples for a pizza or beer or ice cream. The wife of one of the other ambulance drivers told me about an opening for a manicurist maybe coming up at Klip'n'Kurl in the Yankee Plaza, and I figured things might be on the upswing. About time, too.

Getting the dayshift meant Ray had to work weekends. Wednesday and Thursday were his days off. With me not working, it was all the same to us. Once I got a job, we'd manage something. I'd probably have to work Saturdays anyway. In my line of work, Saturday's the big day.

One Wednesday morning about a month and a half after the little Jankowski boy died, Ray and I were sleeping in after a pretty late night in the Ramada Inn lounge when Big Jesse went into his routine and woke us up.

"Sugar-pie, honey-bun (three-four), you know that I love (two) you (four) . . . (one-two-three) cain't he'p mah'se'f (two-three-four) . . . ."

We hadn't heard him in a week or so, and maybe we were still high on Rusty Nails—I don't know. Anyway, it just got to us. We both started laughing, holding our sides and rolling around on the bed. Then Ray began to sing along:

"Ah git all choked-up inside (four) . . . ."

We buried our faces in the pillows so Big Jesse wouldn't hear, next thing I knew Ray buried his face somewhere else, and after that who could sleep?

We were getting up awhile later when I heard her:

"Jesse . . . Jess-eee . . . ."

It wasn't very loud, but she sounded like she was dying. Or in bad pain, at least. I looked at Ray. He listened for a second, then went into the bathroom, like he didn't want me looking at him.

I stayed where I was, waiting, but everything stayed quiet. A couple of minutes went by, then she started again.

I knew Big Jesse was gone. We'd heard him clump down the stairs at least a half-hour before. I wondered if maybe I should go to see what was wrong, but it seemed like that would be butting in. After all, I didn't actually know her. Besides, if she needed help, I figured she'd be making a lot more noise.

"Jesse . . . Jess-eee . . . ."

I turned on the radio, then went and got in the shower with Ray.

I guess I should have expected a blow-up to come sooner or

later. With Ray, I mean. Like he always says, that's bound to happen when you don't talk things out. If you push big problems off to one side, then some little bit of nothing can explode right in front of you. That's how it was with us.

The job finally opened up at Klip'n'Kurl and I got it. The day I was hired, Ray and I decided to celebrate—at home, just the two of us. When he got off work, we went to Shoppersmart and picked out a thick sirloin—enough for four, plus fresh mushrooms, a four-pack of those little shrimp cocktails that come in juice glasses, and a box of frozen éclairs. The tab was going to be huge, and I was worrying about it while we were waiting in the check-out line. I'm not one for spending money I haven't earned yet.

Ray looked at me, grinning, like he could read my mind. "Going to be a big night."

"Expensive," I said.

"I ain't done yet!" He took off and came back just as the cashier was ringing up our order.

"These, too," Ray told her, setting down three cans of artichoke hearts, a dollar eighty-nine apiece, and a box of Schrafft's chocolates.

"Ray—."

"We're celebrating," he said. "Live a little."

On the way home, we stopped to buy a bottle of wine but wound up with champagne instead. Not my idea.

When we got back to the apartment, Ray pushed me toward the bedroom. "I'll take care of everything," he said. "You go slip into something—you know."

I was about to put up an argument, until I saw how happy he was, like a little kid on Christmas Eve, all geared-up.

"Okay. I'll do the cooking, though."

"I'll set you up." He winked, making that sound real sexy.

"We'll just *see* who's set-up, buster!" He started to chase me and I slammed the bedroom door in his face. "Keep your pants on, will you?"

"Anything but that!"

I took my time, putting on this silky hostess-pajama outfit Ray gave me for my birthday, something I never really have much chance to wear. It's pink and has a really low neckline—not exactly my style, but the kind of thing he likes. I think I'm a little too big on top, but Ray says if you've got it, flaunt it. I guess that's okay in private. Besides, it was nice to see him in such a good mood. I sprayed myself with some cologne he says turns him on.

When I came back out, Ray was setting the table. He had the food ready, pans set out on the stove, dishes on the counter. All I'd have to do was light the burners.

In the kitchen I noticed the empty grocery bag, folded and left on the counter next to the two cans of artichokes Ray hadn't opened. The lids of the cans were dusty. I wasn't surprised. At that price, they must sit on the shelf a long time. I picked up the bag and shook it out, looking for the cash register tape. I always save receipts, in case I want to return anything. The bag was empty.

"Ray? Honey?"

"Minute," he yelled from the bedroom.

I looked in the garbage pail under the sink, but it had been emptied out. I put in the fresh bag for a liner.

"You called?" Ray walked into the kitchen, wearing a clean shirt, one of the print ones he let me pick out for him. It had a lot of blue in it and made his eyes look . . . bigger, somehow. Ray has beautiful eyes. I think I fell in love with them before the rest of him. He had combed his hair and put on a gold neckchain I gave him the first year we were together, before I knew he thought jewelry didn't look right on men. The top two buttons of his shirt were open, to show off the chain. I put my arms around him and pressed my face against his chest.

"That's just what I was thinking." Ray slid his hands up and down my slippery pink pajamas. "Mmm."
"Dinner," I said.
"Fine by me. Your party, babe." He started rubbing his nose against my ear. "Do things any order you want."
I pulled away, laughing. "Where's the grocery receipt?"
"What?"
"The little white receipt from the grocery bag," I said. "What happened to it?"
"I just threw the garbage down the chute. Must've been in there, I guess."
"Oh, Ray!"
"Hey, so what?"
I tried not to look at the two cans of artichokes on the counter. "It's just that I save those, hon . . . in case I need to return something."
"At the grocery store?"
"You never know . . . ."
"*You* never know," he said, making his little dry-spit sound.
"Just trying to be careful. That's all."
"Yeah." He looked at me as if I'd kicked him in the stomach, and I realized all of a sudden that the weeks of not talking hadn't done any good. The opposite, in fact. I felt a little sick.
"Forget it, honey," I said. "Not important."
Ray turned around, hunching his shoulders, and that scared me. He wasn't even bothering to argue, to tell me it was important. Important to him. It seemed like he was chalking me off.
We went through with our plans, saying nothing else that night about what was important and what wasn't. There was a lot of food left over. We never made it to the éclairs. I refroze them, even though the package said not to. I would have taken them back to the store—the artichokes and candy, too—if I'd only had the receipt.

We went to bed right after dinner and made love. But it didn't last very long. And I had the strangest feeling—like somebody was watching us. Right there in the room. This doesn't make much sense, but I felt like it was Ray. Him standing next to the bed. And me holding somebody else.

The next morning, Wednesday, we heard Big Jesse in the shower again. We pretended to sleep through the racket. When his steel-toed workboots clomped down the hallway, I started watching the clock, which was on my side of the bed. Behind me, Ray was trying to breathe like somebody who was asleep.

Thirty-five minutes later, she started in:
"Jesse . . . Jess-eee . . . ."

Her voice seemed softer than the times before, but more hurt. Sort of desperate but hopeless, like a person would call for help when they knew nobody was there because they'd already been calling for a long, long time. The quiet spells in-between lasted longer than usual. This time, though, I thought she'd never stop. It reminded me of this dog I had when I was a kid—never barked, but whimpered constantly. Hours at a time. I had it less than a year when it got run over right in front of the house. I was the one who found it by the curb. It looked like a toy, black and fuzzy and not very big, lying in a puddle of red paint. I yelled for my aunt—Lucille, the one who raised me after my Mom took off—and when she saw what was what, she said, "Don't look." But of course I already had.

Anyway, the Jankowski woman whimpered like an animal. I knew Ray heard her, too. And I knew he didn't believe I was asleep, any more than I believed he was. I stayed still anyhow, picturing my dead dog and feeling like I had to throw up.

Finally, when I couldn't take another minute of it, I got up.

"What are you going to do?" Ray asked. He sounded sad and scared.

"Do? Nothing."
"Come here," he said.
"I have to go to the bathroom."
"Come here. Listen."
"What do you think I've been doing?"
"Listen some more." He was practically whispering.
"I can't stand any more," I told him.
"Come here and *listen*." His voice was low and ugly now, not sad or scared. Mean. Not like him.

I picked up Ray's shirt up off the floor and put it on. Then, hugging myself, I walked over and sat stiffly on the edge of the bed. The voice next door seemed to wait until I settled down.

"Jesse . . . Jess-eee . . . ."

"That's what you're afraid of," Ray said.

"I don't know what you're talking about."

His fingers clamped around my wrists like handcuffs, cold and cutting. He hadn't gotten up, but flat on his back, he's still ten times stronger than I am.

"Even Gloria could do better than that," he said. Gloria was his wife. His face had gone tough and dark. Little lumps of muscle stood out below his cheekbones and in his chin.

"Honey, don't—."

"Gloria didn't understand anything, but you—."

Ray sat up in bed and took me by the shoulders. I thought he was going to shake me, or throw me across the room. He's never hit me, but he might have then, except for her. His fingers dug into my upper arms until my eyes watered. "Listen," he said. "You hear that?"

"Honey—."

"Just *listen*, dammit!"

I began to cry, turning my face away from him.

Ray didn't say anything for awhile. I just kept on crying, trying to pull away because he was hurting my arms. But I couldn't get away from him. Finally, he let me go with a shove that nearly landed me on the floor.

"I can't make you see if you won't look," he said.

When I came out of the bathroom, Ray was sitting on the side of the bed, naked, the sheet pulled across his lap. He was staring down at the floor, still listening.

"Honey?" I said it real soft, like we were in the dark and I was trying to tell if he was awake. "Ray?"

"What?" he said, loud.

"There's nothing we can do. We don't know her."

"Don't you think I know that?"

He still looked like he might want to hit me. I stayed by the bathroom door. "What's the matter, then?"

"You can't pretend like she's not there."

He lay down again. The sheet fell to the floor as he stretched himself, kitty-corner, all the way across the bed until his fingertips were touching the wall. He stayed like that, reaching, his bluish fingers pressed against the shadowy brown pattern of the wallpaper. His behind, sticking up at an angle, looked smooth and white as could be.

I wanted to touch him. He looked so helpless, stretched out naked that way. And I guess I never really noticed before how little difference there is between a man's body and a little kid's. I tried to think of something to say, but sometimes there just isn't any use talking. I knew what Ray was thinking: he was wishing that wall wasn't there. But I was glad it was. The difference between us . . . I guess that's what it comes down to.

The following week, I started my new job. That was about a month ago. It seems to be working out fine, so far. I like the other girls and the salon is busy. The owner, Tony, says I'm good for business, because I'm friendly and remember the customers' names and all.

WALLS

It was too bad, how I happened to find work just at the time Ray's vacation was coming up. But the hospital has to plan employees' vacations way in advance, and I couldn't pass up a steady job. Besides, Ray and I talked it over and decided it wouldn't hurt if he got away for a few weeks. He was all wound up.

As much as Ray doesn't want anything to do with his ex-wife, he's going to have to deal with her—like he says, stop pretending she's not there—if he wants to see his kid. And he does. I can hardly blame him. It's a little girl. She's five now, in kindergarten, and her name is Tiffany Ann. Ray hasn't seen her since she was a baby.

He told me about the kid for the first time when I was driving him to the airport that night. It came as a pretty big shock. Before then, he'd just said he was flying out to Seattle to "visit family." I figured that meant his folks and two brothers who live out there. I've never met them. Anyway, the fewer questions asked, the better, seeing how things were with us.

So when Ray first gave me the full story, it really threw me. A kid—I mean, how could he keep something like that from me all this time? He tried to pass it off like it wasn't all that important. I could tell he was afraid I'd blow up or something. But I didn't. If he has a kid, I can't tell him not to care, can I? Besides, we had enough trouble. With him leaving, I didn't want to get into saying anything I'd only want to take back later. I didn't want him to, either. Still, I felt like bawling. Not that it would have changed anything.

I went inside the airport with him, but they wouldn't let me walk him out to the gate. We had to say goodbye in front of that electronic doorway they have to make sure people aren't carrying weapons.

Ray had two big suitcases, and I got kind of queasy, looking at how much stuff he was taking with him. He grunted when he had to lift his bags up on the conveyor belt. They slipped out of sight behind these black rubber flaps. Then I could see x-rays of them on a little T.V. screen in the wall, moving away too fast for me to tell one thing from another. A lot of folded clothes, I guess, and something that might have been a hairbrush on top. Everything was gray.

There were guards motioning people through the wired passage, telling everybody to empty their pockets and take off their watches. Another guard checked tickets and kept an eye on the rest of us.

A lot of people were waiting to go through behind Ray, so we couldn't say much. When it was his turn to go, Ray held on to me really hard for a second. I put my arms around him and felt the springy hair under the thin material of his shirt. Then he pulled away. I never got a chance to see how his face looked.

"Maybe you could take a picture of Tiffany Ann and send it to me. A Polaroid or something? I'll put it up in the shop. We have a bulletin board."

"Sure," Ray said, over his shoulder.

"Call and let me know when you're getting back. I'll be here."

"You bet."

I watched him walk down the long corridor, hurrying between all these strangers and suitcases. The walls were plastered with posters of Las Vegas showgirls and Fisherman's Wharf and the Virgin Islands. Ray's gate was the last one on the left, way down at the end. All of a sudden he seemed so small and far away.

"Don't look," I said to myself as he went through the door. "Don't look."

But of course I already had.

POTIONS

POTIONS

> "When the King saw the blood on the Queen's garments, he believed that she had allowed the child to be carried off by a wild animal and he was overwhelmed with anger. He caused a high tower to be built, into which neither sun nor moon could penetrate. Then he ordered his wife to be shut up in it and the door walled up. She was to stay there seven years without eating or drinking, so she would gradually pine away. But two angels from heaven, in the shape of white doves, came to her, bringing food twice a day. . . ."
>
> "The Pink"
Grimm's Fairy Tales

I hear them talking about me, out in the corridor, using the indulgent tones parents use to confess their children's sins.

"She still won't eat."

I cannot tell whether they are amused or annoyed. Perhaps they are not sure themselves.

"She drinks the water."

"Yes. But nothing else."

I like it here. They have moved me to the quietest side of the quietest floor. The ones who screech and shatter things are segregated on other wings, for we are grouped here according to symptom. Silence is what I have in common with the other occupants of this corridor. And hunger, possibly. But I cannot be certain of that.

The doctor comes.

"How—?"

"She still won't eat," they tell him, clucking with dismay.

"Nothing?"

"The water. That's all."

I am gratified. Their annoyance seems to be gaining the upper hand. I distinguish myself with their annoyance.

"We'll have to try the I.V. again," the doctor says.

"She'll only pull it out."

"If we turn our backs on her, yes. She must be watched."

You see? I have distinguished myself. I bear watching.

The doctor goes. His feet tap down the corridor with precision. I know the tread is his, for it is masculine: opinionated and terse. The nurses skim on ambiguous soles, their steps neither here nor there. Only their voices give them away.

"What are we going to do with her?"

They swoop into my room like doves, high-breasted and cooing. Their white-winged caps dispense a certain foolish charm. It undermines them when they mean to be stern with me, their charm. But they know enough not to be stern first thing in the morning. They are captivating.

"Good morning, good morning . . . good morning!" They flutter around my bed.

I incline my head toward them.

"Good morning, Mrs. Bellefleur! And how are we today?"

(Do they actually call me that—"we"—or is it something I make up to suit my own purposes? "We" is the pet name I have always had for myself. A private endearment. I need to feel at home here.)

The younger nurse, a sturdy Norwegian girl whose ash-blond hair never stays pinned beneath her cap, wraps the blood-pressure belt around my upper arm and pumps away at her little rubber ball. There is a wide jade band on her finger, mottled, the colors of moss and lichen. I feel like a balloon she is blowing up with her squeezes. But before I burst, she stops. The air whooshes out of me. My arm is pulsating as she tears the strip from it.

"Normal," she says. The other one nods, writes something on a chart.

A cold thermometer is thrust under my tongue. I do not resist. It feels good to have something in my mouth. Once they left a tongue depressor on my bedside table. All day I gnawed on it, until splinters were caught in my teeth.

The thermometer is snatched away, held up to the light. "Normal," the Norwegian says again. The older nurse sighs softly, the corners of her mouth curling as she enters the notation. I see I have forced her into a false position. She does not find me normal at all. Her brown eyes darken with resentment. She is my accomplice.

"Your breakfast tray will be right along." She smiles at me, carrying her duplicity to the limit. "Are you going to eat something for us this morning?"

My smile is as convincing as hers: I scarcely move my lips.

"For them." That is an accidental truth she let slip. The food they bring and try to force into my fingers and throat is only for them. For them.

We are not going to eat.

In the beginning, the weakness is dreadful. A bodily matter. Desire persists after the ability to effect anything dwindles. Will dies hard, and we suffer greatly at its hands, in its clutches. But this passes. Eventually, weakness invades will, subdues it. And when will's grip finally grows lax, the weakness is absolutely wonderful.

We are feeling wonderful now. There is nothing we can do. Now we lie here for hours on end, floating. Not minding. Not wanting to do anything at all. The bed is like the Dead Sea . . . viscous, tepid, buoyant. Awash in an amniotic fluid of uncaring, we find it wonderful—being so helpless, without weight.

The doctor returns and enters our room. "Good morning. Good morning." He is not like a dove. The flapping white wings of his coat do not mislead us. He walks on the balls of his feet. Perhaps he hopes to fool us by disguising his footsteps.

He slithers through the door and coils himself at the foot of our bed. We recognize his species.

"How are we today?"

(Does he really put it quite that way?)

We incline our head toward him.

The doctor lifts our hospital gown and looks askance at what is underneath. He presses a chilled medallion to our chest, a brief award for the valor which distinguishes us.

He listens. Twists his small head with a sinuous grace. Hoods his eyes. His upper parts puff up like an adder's.

"What are we going to do with you?"

He removes the medal before it has even warmed to us. We are again without honor in our own country. But the extent to which we do not mind is wonderful.

"I understand you still refuse to eat." The doctor's grimness is a formality.

We incline our head away from him, nuzzling closer to our precious weakness.

"We shall have to do something radical, I'm afraid."

We remain wonderfully unperturbed. Needles are nothing to us. Needles are all his species knows.

The doctor goes, gliding on the balls of his feet. We hear him bring down his heels in the corridor. Our implacability frustrates him. We suspect he grimaces, baring venomous fangs on the other side of the door. The picture amuses us, and we smile weakly. Our head leans to one side, and when we lick our lips, they have a salty taste. We look forward to lunching on crushed ice in its own juices.

We do not sleep. But neither are we quite awake much of the time. We are at sea level, precisely, which makes it difficult to take in the general topography. We drift, allowing the mountains their attempt to come to us. They will not succeed. Our will is not required to keep the peaks at a distance. We have a distance of our own.

It is presumed that we sleep. The presumption suits us. Belief in our sleep permits us to listen, to slip needles from our veins when backs are turned. It is true that our eyes remain closed much of the time. But we do not sleep. We listen.

"Have they reached her husband yet?"

"Well, not exactly. I mean, they've found him, but . . . ."

They are whispering.

"You mean he still won't come?"

"He won't even talk when doctor phones."

"They ought to call the police."

"For what? He agrees to pay the bills."

"It isn't right."

"Doctor says he's crazy with grief . . . off the deep end."

They continue to talk. The nurses love to talk. I can hear them perfectly, but I can no longer understand them. It is as if they have lapsed into a foreign language. Their syntax eludes me. I have no vocabulary, have no . . . .

We do not concern ourselves with conversation, past a certain point.

They think we do not know what has happened. They think we are in the dark. That we have cultivated a selective strain of amnesia to block out personal misfortune. "Our tragedy," they call it.

They could not be farther from the truth. We know exactly what's what, what we're doing, what we've done.

We have, to some extent, been disowned.

Being an essentially decent man, our provider naturally assumes financial responsibility for our care. The fact that he has extensive insurance coverage is beside the point. He would pay just as promptly out-of-pocket. He believes in the thirty-day remittance, makes no allowance for the outstanding balance, the carrying charge. A person of excellent character and credit rating, our provider has disowned us. And his irreproachability is central to the drama, intrinsic to our denouément. The blamelessness of the man of the house counterbalances our own liability, furnishing our story's essential element of tension.

Do we create the impression, false as our doctor's bedside footwork, that we are unwinding merely one more tawdry saga of burnt potroasts and lukewarm infidelities?

We hope not.

Actually, though our dowry was modest, it did include a certain culinary flair and a strict ethical code. These contributed toward our upkeep for seven years. Our provider was betrayed neither with frozen convenience foods nor with keys to cheap motel rooms. Our devotion was without question. We went so far as to bake our own bread.

The single delicate imbalance in the arrangement was chemical, a matter of hormones, or chromosomes perhaps. It was a grave deficiency, however: our inability to conceive an heir.

We were aggrieved and mystified. Our obstinate body shamed us. Doggedly we consulted men of science, submitted to clinical indignities, but no organic cause for our infertility came to light. Ultimately, we had to assume some sort of spiritual flaw—petulant ovaries or a mean-spirited womb.

We recognized the validity of what was implied about us. We must confess that from our very wedding night, we had found it troublesome to bear up under the weight of our provider's excellence. Some critical mass obstructed our passion. And the failure of passion had obviously rendered us barren.

"It is hardly your fault," our provider insisted.

We knew better.

Comprehending the gravity of our failing, we turned with a desperate innocence to seers, oracles, witches, and wizards.

POTIONS

We whispered incantations and lapsed eagerly into spells. And then, on the best advice, we turned to potions.

It seemed so simple, a fortuitous convergence of science, magic, and commonsense. Drink this . . . swallow that . . . at bedtime. The secret was to relax, loosening the self-centered tension so fiercely barring entry to our womb.

In hope, we complied with instructions, acquiring a taste for the liquids and capsules which made us more hospitable. We learned to love dusk and its aftermath. We hoarded a cache of vials in a mirrored cabinet and dreamed all day of nighttime sorceries. Our spiritual dimensions seemed to expand. We chatted on the most familiar terms with our household gods.

And eventually our incantations were answered: after years of marriage and many potions, we conceived.

We knew the moment it happened. (We insist upon this: it is our right, our story.) It was a night in midwinter. The man of the house was soundless and determined. Bare lilac branches scratched like witches' fingernails across the frosted window of the bedroom. There was no moon. We floated under our provider's insistent weight, eyes open to a darkness which was complete and inevitable. We did not argue with the blackness. Instead, for the first time, we found favor with it. We were rewarded: something deep within us gave way, opening up wide, generous, unresisting. It was done. And we knew.

Nine months later, in the last days of the harvest, on the Feast of All Souls, a son was born.

And there was great rejoicing.

We apologize for trailing off. We are just so wonderfully weak. We tire easily.

The doves are cooing in the hall again, preparing to bring us food.

"Is she on the I.V. yet?"

"It's on the way up now."
"Who can we get to stay with her?"
Whom.
Not that it matters. Any of it. They will bob through life, little white caps scattering hairpins and faulty grammar and false heartiness in their wake. And we can surely outwit anyone assigned to sit with us. The weakness makes us rather crafty, if we may say so.
Where were we?
Yes, we were speaking of the son, whose birth caused great joy. And of his father, an excellent man. And of his mother, who, by the time the child was born, was devoted to secret potions, an addiction acquired under the auspices of love, relaxation, and purposeful darkness.
The baby favored his father: an excellent boychild in every way, so beautiful that the angels wept for envy and the stars hid for shame. (Or so his parents liked to think—the child's life having enlarged their imaginations.)
The mother, like all new mothers, marvelled at the miracle of her son's tiny toes and the smell of his skin. She brushed the reddish-gold hairs on his head with a silver-backed brush whose bristles were softer than feathers, and she was sometimes so overwhelmed with love for him that she wept. Awed and terrified at her son's perfection, she continued to swallow the potions she believed had made a mother of her. The liquids and capsules staved off wild beasts, witches, evil spells which meant to harm the child. The contents of the hidden vials sedated jealous angels and wove a platinum scrim of safekeeping around the baby and herself. She relaxed.
And then one day, safe behind the scrim, the mother and her baby slumbered on a high, wide bed fit for the chamber of a King and Queen. The bed had a richly embroidered coverlet of eggshell color, and many pillows with lace edges and satin ribbons. The scalloped hem of a dust-ruffle dipped to the floor.

POTIONS

The child, who lacked for nothing, had a cradle of his very own. The cradle was extremely old, for it had belonged to his father and his grandfather before him. The cradle was fashioned from lustrous cherry wood, with high, spindly sides and carved rails. It took no more than a flick of a mother's slender wrist to set it rocking gently.

To the father, the cradle seemed an excellent place for the child's safekeeping. The man would stand beside it in the night, watching over his son's sleep and indulging his own imagination, while the mother was weaving dreams in the big bed.

During the days, however, the mother took the child from the cradle and kept him in the high, wide, white-covered bed with her. She knew the scrim enclosed them there. She would drift into sleep, her body curved around her tiny son, and relinquish belief in the harm that could come to him. She relaxed.

On the day the boychild turned one hundred and fifty-seven days old, the sky darkened. It was early afternoon, and snow began to fall in tufts from a gunmetal sky on the other side of the window, beyond the platinum scrim. The mother swallowed her potion and carried the child to her bed. Then she lay down on her side, curving gently toward him: a pearl, small, gleaming, perfect. She loosely fitted herself around him, like a shell, half-open. He was already sleeping, his pink fists knotting the corners of a little bud-sprigged comforter his godmother had stitched for him.

The child was safe.

The mother slept.

She awoke in the middle of the afternoon, facing the window. She noticed first that the snow had stopped. In the bottom corner of the window, a branch of the lilac bush cracked like a whip in the wind. It was rimed with frost, glittery with sunlight. It came as such a surprise to her, seeing the sun . . . .

Son.

She sat up quickly, but without jarring the bed. There was a confusing ache behind her eyes which permitted her to believe, for a moment, that she was still dreaming.

The miniature flowered quilt was draped over the edge of the high, wide mattress. But the baby, her son, was not beneath it. The baby was not on the bed. The baby was no longer within the scrim of safekeeping.

From behind the semi-opaque folds of the potions, she saw him: her perfect boychild askew on the floor far below. His tiny neck had snapped like a frozen lilac twig. His fists had not unclenched in death. They had turned from pink to lavender. And his violet eyes were closed. Their color was never seen again.

We hear the squeak and screech and rattle in the corridor. We hear the cooing. They are coming, wheeling the hanging bottles on their tripod frame to us. The lowest-common-denominator nourishment they hope to force into our lavender veins. They will not get far with us. We find the means to outwit them each time.

"Is she sleeping?"

"Dead to the world."

You see how easy it is to outwit them.

"I heard her husband called this morning."

"He'll be coming, then?"

"No. He left a different address. For the bills, he said."

"What a bastard."

These nurses—they are like children.

Sometimes we are tempted to explain things to them. Their foolishness frustrates us, even at a distance. But we are so wonderfully weak that talk is out of the question. We have cause to be grateful.

The man we married is not a bastard. Definitely not. In fact, we would say that his conduct, considering the circumstances, is irreproachable. He has left us to our own devices. His turning away from us is a measure of his excellent sensibilities, the delicacy of his manners.

We turn over on our side, pulling the white hospital blankets up to our ears. They muffle the sounds in the corridor. We are facing the window, and we see that it is snowing again. Or still. We lose track of time in our weakness.

There is a pecking at the door. We wrap our arms tightly around us beneath the covers. It is a part of our task to create obstacles and diversions for them, when they approach us with their needles and upended bottles of clear, colorless food. On our better days, we can prolong the search and seizure of a vein to nearly an hour. Our modes of resistance, even when we are weak, are wonderfully subtle.

The door opens. We hold perfectly still, buried under a drift of blankets. Our arms are pinned to our sides. It pleases us to feel how our bones have begun to assert themselves. Metal rattles near our bed, rubber wheels skid on the floor. We open one eye to a slit and see the bottle looming above us, swaying slightly. Our enemy.

We relax, wonderfully weak, still as death. Let them try whatever they know. Let their arcane rites be performed over us. Even inert, we are a match for them. They have no answer for death. Only arguments.

Concentration is the secret of our dominance. They are distracted here, have other things on their minds. The will to live disables their efforts, dooms them. They possess no answer. They are bluffing.

We, on the other hand, are singular in our focus. Clearheaded. We have found our answer. It is unassailable. Nothing remains for us to do but lie here, defeating them, until we slide, finally, over the edge.

SNOWBIRD

SNOWBIRD

The old man would doze before the nattering television set in his California apartment and dream of her—his daughter, somewhere in New Hampshire, where there surely would be snow. He would dream up great drifts, snow piling high around his daughter near Franconia. She would play in it, shaping grandchildren for him with her blue, womanly fingers. Button noses, eyes made out of coal, corncob pipes for playthings . . . grandchildren, something he dreamed up.

When he would wake, the old man would walk out on anyone who happened to be there with him—Archie Bunker, Merv Griffin, Morley Safer. He had even walked out on Walter Cronkite, before Walter Cronkite walked out on him. Once he had walked out on Sir Kenneth Clark. He knew trepidation only when he dreamed.

The old man would launch himself from his Naugahyde recliner, sailing over green swells of shag carpet like a decrepit dinghy on crosscurrents. He was springing leaks, he knew. His eyes had acquired a habit of purposeless trickling. Strange fluids flowed through his lungs. The old man disliked his need for handkerchiefs. He bought the kind that looked like bandanas, filling them with phlegms and brackish waters. More often than not, he would throw them away rather than wash them. His daughter, he felt, would have approved of the extravagance. She was impractical.

Deborah. He pictured her, an enchanting child, as he tacked unsteadily past the television. In fact, Deborah had not been a particularly enchanting child. Her voice had matched her mother's for stridency before her baby-mouth formed words. A pale and lumpish little girl, nearsighted, her hands and feet over-large. But the father, old and widowed now, clung to his retouched portraits of her. Belief in his daughter's enchantment helped to distract him from the ballast he was losing as the years towed him under.

Dreams of New Hampshire snows and his baby's charms intact, the old man would strip naked behind his bathroom door. Balancing on one foot like a cartoon flamingo, he worked a brown knit bathing suit up his withered thighs and over his picked-clean shanks. He told himself he would rather be too skinny than too fat. His torso was flat as a farm boy's. His ribs stuck out at brave angles. His daughter was going to get hefty if she wasn't careful. The old man's choicest contempt was reserved for self-indulgence.

The pool was balmy. He shared it with the occupants of seven other apartments, but no one else came out at night. The old man paddled back and forth, making surveys with his unreliable, dripping eyes. The desert air was cool after sunset. His skin, shrinking as he left the tepid water, reminded him of a lifetime of New Hampshire mornings, reluctant crawlings from lukewarm beds. Rains were brief and seldom here, but the drops seemed to pierce him like poison darts. It had been an awful surprise at first, that rain fell at all in the desert. But he had learned to appreciate breaks in the weather's monotony. Clouds appeared like messengers from the different world beyond the mountains.

The old man's evening swim was a necessary habit, a bedtime story he told himself. Its purpose was not entertainment: he knew its ending by heart. He would float on his back in the deep end, watching the night sky, and picture his daughter, asleep under thick white covers behind a range of peaked drifts. New Hampshire.

Afterwards, centering himself on his king-size Posturpedic mattress, once more the old man would conjure up shiny-eyed grandchildren. They would dance in his dreams like sugarplums, swaying and dipping, as he sternly advised his daughter on their care and feeding and financial interests. When he awoke, he remembered to mind his own business. Remembered there were no enchanting children. Just as well. The girl had never even learned to look after herself.

"Daddy?"
Deborah's voice never made it to California in one piece. It seemed to get damaged in transit. The old man wanted to blame AT&T, to register a complaint. But he could not help blaming Deborah: her long-distance tone estranged them.
"Daughter," he said.
"How *are* you, Daddy?"
"Fine just fine." 'Daddy'—too old for such talk. Trying, he supposed, to make up for holding out on him, withholding grandchildren. A shoddy substitution.
"You're feeling all right?" She always called first thing in the morning, sounding vaguely alarmed, as if in doubt he had lasted the night.
"Of course I am." He regretted snapping, tried to mask his crankiness. "How are *you*, Daughter?"
"Oh, fine. But it's so *cold* here."
"Why don't you come out for a visit?" The question was rhetorical. The old man knew she would not consider it.
"Maybe next year." Three thousand miles of dangerous wire dismantled her laugh. The old man felt its remnants lodge in his throat. He coughed.
"Is there anything you need?"
"Nothing."
"How about some oatmeal cookies?"
Her wistfulness was not lost on him. "I wouldn't turn them down," he said.
"I'll bake some tomorrow."
"Fine."

The last time she sent cookies, they had arrived in fragments. He had eaten them with a soup spoon, over many evenings, after his swims.

"Daughter?"

"Yes, Daddy?"

"What about Elliot?"

"What about him?"

Her husband had fled her over-large hands and feet, her harsh consonants, for Tampa. The old man figured New Hampshire winters hadn't helped matters. Elliot was tropical, exotic, foolish. He might have been a myna bird, a parrot, in love with his own voice.

It had been no surprise to the old man to get a fool for a son-in-law. No point wasting regret on the inevitable. The real disappointment was the unexpected ceiling on the son-in-law's foolishness. The old man had hoped the young one could be tricked into fertilizing eggs in the North country before flying south. Both father and daughter had underestimated Elliot's survival instinct. The exotic bird had left no tracks.

"Daddy?"

"What's that?"

"Did you hear me?"

"Sorry. Bad connection," he muttered.

"*I said I haven't heard from Elliot.*" Deborah was shouting. A passing cloud subdued the brightness in the old man's living room.

"Is he sending you money?"

"His lawyer is."

"You'll go through with it then—the divorce?"

"I guess." She sounded bewildered.

"Enough?"

"What?"

"The money he's sending—is it enough?"

"I'm looking for a job."

The old man said nothing. A vision of his grandchildren, melting, passed before his eyes. He compressed his lips.

"I *love* you, I said . . . ."

"How's that?"

"I love you, Daddy." Deborah's voice quit trying to go the distance. She sounded almost . . . .

Enchanting.

"Goodbye, Daughter," the old man said, taking matters into his own hands.

A widow lived next door. She hated the sun, stayed indoors between ten and three, defacing her cheeks with rouge. Her throat looked white and clammy, like the underbelly of some repulsive fish.

Every Monday, the widow borrowed the old man's car to do her weekly marketing. Every Tuesday she brought him a pot of homemade soup: bean, lentil, cabbage, chicken rice, or vegetable. And a small pudding: rice, bread, tapioca, or coconut. The soups were unsalted, the puddings suspicious shades of yellow. The widow insisted that the old man call her Myra. He never asked her to call him anything. She called him Mr. Gunther. His name was Herbert.

The old man subscribed to a good neighbor policy based on fences. An isolationist by conviction, a natural keeper of distances, he kept his distance from the widow next door, from anyone who resided too close for his comfort. He had been dismayed, when he arrived from the East, to find no fencing in these new communities, an oversight of inexperience. He secured his own borders, however. After a few half-hearted attempts to cross them, his neighbors left him alone.

"Snowbirds" the winter residents of the California desert called themselves, as if they could make their migratory status more tenable by mocking it. They swooped down in flocks around swimming pools in late autumn, setting up makeshift nests near the golf courses of Palm Springs, Palm Desert, Rancho Mirage, Cathedral City, Indio. Their ersatz hale-and-heartiness seemed a bit desperate: they were trying to drown out the endangerment of their own species by sheer volume. They bathed and twittered and strutted, doing their best to deflect attention from their clipped wings.

The old man was not popular with the Snowbirds, was nobody's favorite. He did not play golf, would not even try, refused to discuss it. He turned his back on pool-side bridge games, avoided sharing the hot tub with other bodies, withheld commiseration over arthritis—even though his own was obvious. The old man discouraged first-name-basis dealings. He deleted his daughter from conversation, relegating her to New England, where she belonged. Taciturnity reaped rewards: the Snowbirds left him to his own devices.

Exclusion suited the old man. Having foraged among the leavings of his life to piece together a kind of contentment, he was not about to brook interference. But the Glendenning woman, the widow next-door, was an interference. The old man wished she would simply take his car keys and leave him be. Wished she would keep her soups and puddings to herself. He ate them, of course, but only to get rid of them.

Her tentative knock rattled his door at a quarter past ten. Fifteen minutes later than usual. The noise was less disruptive than his anticipation of it. The old man felt out of sorts.

"Good morning . . . Myra." His mouth twisted in distaste at using her name. He noted that she looked rather dishevelled. This did not interest him, except that it was unlike her. The spots of color on her sagging cheeks were misaligned. Her ridiculous top-knot was untidy. Stray mouse-colored hairs straggled down her neck.

"Mr. Gunther."

As always, the woman carried her soup pot and the small covered custard dish in a frayed wicker basket. She held it out to him. His part of the ritual was to accept her offerings, remove them to the kitchen, return the empty basket. She hovered half in, half out of his apartment, while the old man did what was expected of him. She took the basket. He waited for her to go.

"Oh, dear," the widow said.

Her voice wobbled, startling the old man. Disdain flickered on his face, but she appeared oblivious to it as she rummaged in the pocket of her pantsuit. The diamond-patterned cloth of her jacket made the old man queasy, and he looked down quickly. Straw sandals, gaudy as a Carmen Miranda headdress. Toenails painted like a tart's. Calloused toes curling under, wisely trying to hide. The old man devoted his full attention to despising the widow's feet.

"Oh, dear," she cried again. "I *do* apologize!"

Looking up, he saw his car keys dangling from a shocking pink-tipped claw. She had taken the keys yesterday morning.

"My word, I'm so embarrassed. What must you think of me?"

"Please," he said.

"It's just not like me at all, forgetting a thing like this!" Then the woman appalled him by breaking into noisy weeping. Her narrow shoulders heaved.

"It doesn't matter," the old man muttered.

"It does. It *does*." Her top-knot bobbed in time to her agitation. "Unforgiveable."

"The car was not needed."

". . . not myself at all today . . . ."

"What is it?" he asked, damning himself for the question. "Is something wrong?"

"I can't—." Mrs. Glendenning shook her head and backed into the corridor. "Please excuse me, I . . . ."

Her own door clicked shut, like teeth snapping off the end of a loose thread.

The old man stood staring into the dim hallway for a moment. A spray of plastic orchids anchored to a heart-shaped straw shield was affixed to the widow's door. Excess. Frippery. The loud clothing and the lack of self-control . . . the woman really was unforgiveable. Intolerable. He should have known better than to get involved with her.

Herbert Gunther shook his head as he went to hang his keys on the hook above the kitchen sink, where they belonged. "A place for everything . . . ."

It simply confounded him, the way some people permitted disorder to take over their lives.

A high wind came up in the afternoon and blew the Snowbirds from the side of the pool. The old man set out to take a walk, but the dust was everywhere, obscuring the snowcapped mountains. A *New York Times*, several days old, flapped on the walk. Then it was drawn up into the sky and never reappeared, like a kite severed from its string.

He sauntered by the mailboxes, but his was empty. The old man pretended not to notice. Returning to his apartment, he decided to take a nap, although he had done nothing to earn it. Normally he was quite strict with himself about such things.

As his defenses lowered under an onslaught of drowsiness, he thought, "I am getting old."

He dreamed he was in New Hampshire, growing short of breath as he shovelled a path through the snow to his daughter's door. He awoke in California with a stitch in his left side. Someone was at his door. He knew it would be the widow. He was too groggy to mind very much.

"Come in," the old man called loudly, righting his reclining chair.

Myra Glendenning had restored her hair and her cheeks, changed her clothing and shoes. Only her smile was not properly arranged.

She crossed the old man's threshhold gingerly. She shut the door behind her, but kept hold of its pistol-shaped handle. He looked at her hand, its bony grip nearly transparent and mottled with violet, and wondered what had ever become of real doorknobs, the kind whose simple round contours filled the palm, withstood generations of comings and goings. Doorknobs of porcelain, alabaster, glass. For a moment, California seemed to him the source of all the spoilage and loss he had had the gumption to ignore in his lifetime.

"I must apologize, Mr. Gunther. I—."

"No need," the old man said.

"But I want to explain. It wasn't the keys—."

"I would have asked if I'd needed them."

". . . trouble . . . my family . . . I'm just upset."

"Of course." The old man did not want to hear, and the woman knew it. "Will you sit down?" he asked.

"No, I won't stay but a moment." Her eyes were about to overflow again, and his stomach tightened. He sought refuge in her shoes, seemly espadrilles. He approved of them. The old man approved, nearly always, of navy blue. And brown. It relieved him to find the widow's toes respectably covered. "My grandson," she murmured.

"Trouble," the old man said, her reformed feet making him agreeable.

"Leukemia." She whispered the word like a secret.

Children.

Melting.

Spoilage.

The old man looked into the watery blue eyes, his own shock

outdoing hers. He had no right to the terror he felt, and he shook his head, ashamed.

Myra Glendenning rubbed her rouged cheek, ruining her own artistry. The old man realized his stare was indelicate. He moved to the plate glass window and gazed outside. The pool was whipped to a froth, an aquamarine confection. Newspapers wrapped themselves around the stringy trunks of date palms, impaled their rumpled remains on spiked hedges. Off in the distance, a bale of tumbleweed advanced on a putting green.

When the old man turned around again, the widow had gone. He remained at the window, waiting for the pearl-crested mountains to reappear.

He made a dinner of her soup, forgetting to be irritated by its blandness. He considered the rice custard as well, but that seemed too much to demand of himself, even as a sympathetic gesture. He left his soup bowl in the sink, unwashed.

The television set was on the fritz. The nightly news came and went, losing its distinct edges as intermittent flurries crossed the screen. The windstorm must have downed a cable somewhere. Children were being murdered in Atlanta, video parents smirking over fluoride tests and peanut butter jars. The old man, tiring of his disgust, allowed the messages to bypass him.

After awhile, he lowered the volume and listened to noises from the next apartment. The widow was fixing dinner. Pots and pans rattled. He wondered if she would actually eat, or if she was merely making a pretense of it. Her phone rang once. Then there was quiet.

The wind abated at ten o'clock. Listening intently for sounds from the next apartment, the old man assured himself that he was only waiting to hear the shrieks and wails of air resume. Nothing happened. At last, he pushed a lever on the arm of his chair. Its back slid forward and launched him.

The carpet yielded under his feet like sponge. He snapped off the television and took his still-damp swim trunks into the small, windowless bathroom, where he urinated and undressed in darkness.

The caretaker had forgotten—or perhaps not bothered, with the storm—to turn on the underwater lights in the pool. The old man was pleased: the blackness was to his liking. He swam three lengths in a slow, even crawl. Small, unseen things floated beside him in the water, brushing his limbs. He tried to scare himself with half-formed images of live creatures—snakes, poisonous amphibians, desert rats. But imagination failed him. He could fabricate nothing more terrible than shredded newsprint, candy wrappers, bits of tumbleweed. Disappointed, he hefted himself up the steps at the pool's shallow end.

The widow's lights were still on. Late, for her. Her drapes were always drawn at dusk. But not tonight . . . not herself, she said. Dripping, shivering, barefoot, the old man passed her picture window, swerving closer than necessary to her patio. He pretended the apartment was part of the natural landscape. Like a casual sightseer, he peered in.

The Glendenning apartment was a duplicate of his own. All its fundamental features were identical: pea-green carpet, formica counters, eggshell walls meant to look like stucco. Her living room was no less cramped and square than his, its imitation Mediterranean furniture as slick and cumbersome. But the woman had made such an infernal fuss of things that the old man's vision blurred. A debris of pictures and potted begonias and ruffled lampshades disoriented him. The coffee table was cluttered to a baroque confusion. The old man felt like a witness to some unspeakable private act.

He and the widow had lived side by side for years. Five, was it? No, closer to seven. Nearly eight years since his wife had died, taking the secrets of her rich and spicy soups, her self-indulgent desserts, her sharp-tongued jokes and practical outlook with her. Deborah had already wed the fool by then. The old man, who had not yet understood that he was old, had closed his accounting office and moved to California. Time to ease up, before his hand was forced. It would do him good to live in a place where he could see the snow without feeling it. Nothing to hold him in the East. He had lived in this apartment, then brand new, for less than a year when the Glendenning woman had moved in next door.

Out by the pool that winter, the Snowbirds had picked over her history, sifting through the known and the invented, scratching for satisfying morsels. A widow, well-off but not rich. Two married sons. A grandchild on the way. When her husband, a manufacturer, developed heart trouble, he swore he'd die before selling the business. He was as good as his word. After a decent interval, Myra Glendenning put the business and the house in East Lansing on the market and moved to the desert. En route she refurbished her wardrobe with light fabrics and cheerful colors.

The Snowbirds were not unkind to the widow, but she did not hold their interest. Lacking fortune, golf handicap, automobile, and suntan, Myra Glendenning fell somewhere outside their experience, somewhere below their standards. She was invited to the sizable parties, for the Snowbirds knew what it was to be alone, and she did play a passable bridge game. The widow seemed content, even grateful, to be held in the loose embrace of the outer circle.

From the first, Myra clearly had intended to befriend the old man. Perhaps she merely meant to be neighborly. Being lonely herself, she may have assumed he was too. Regardless, he told himself, best to nip such overtures in the bud. He detected disappointment in the droop of her shoulders when he rebuffed her, but eventually she seemed to respect his boundaries, to stop taking them personally. The old man considered the widow a fussbudget. No doubt she thought the same of him. But at least they both knew where they stood. He congratulated himself on the fence he had improvised. Its only chinks were his car keys, her soup pot. He had learned to tolerate those. Until today.

Today she had crossed the line of demarcation, the old man thought angrily. Violated their comfortable treaty. The widow should never have let him see her in such a state. Inconsiderate of her, allowing her grief to seep through their common wall, staining his private enclave . . . .

Now, however, spying on his neighbor's sorrow defused the old man's fury.

Naked, Myra Glendenning sat in a straight-backed chair, hugging herself. An ornate barricade of pillows and family portraits and music boxes, knitting bags and knick-knacks and candy dishes enclosed her. Metallic light spilled across the floor from the television, but the woman was not looking toward the screen. She was not looking at her astonishing hoard of trinkets. In fact, she seemed to be looking at nothing at all.

The riot of color the old man had always found so unsettling had broken up, fallen away. Stripped of scarlet patches, the woman's cheeks were ragged. Her hair had come unwound and listed to one side of her head. Her exposed skull, ancient and fragile, shocked the old man more profoundly than her nakedness, the loose-hanging breasts, the reptilian scar-tissue coiled on her abdomen. He realized suddenly what a blessing the woman's protective colorations had been. The glimpse of her natural state was like a steep and sudden drop in the dark.

All at once the old man's weight was beyond him. His hands flew out ahead of him, as if to break a fall. He had begun to stumble toward his own door when he noticed the widow's feet:

Bright pink slippers like oversized powderpuffs. Slippers exactly like those his daughter had worn for years. Perhaps still did. Deborah. Perhaps his daughter still plodded across cold New England floorboards at night on huge pink plush feet . . . .

For several seconds, the old man was paralyzed. He could not recall how to breathe. Helpless, staring through his neighbor's window, he longed for his own bed, where he could promise himself he was only dreaming an old fool's dreams. He could not take his eyes from the widow's feet.

Finally, exerting an icy will, he exhaled sharply. The lure of his own bed, his door, his decorous rooms released him. Equal to his own weight again, the old man turned and, with cold stiff fingers, he drummed lightly on the glass.

Myra did not react visibly to the sound.

Herbert Gunther knocked again, more firmly. "Myra," he said, as if nothing stood between them. She lowered her head, and he waited. "Myra?"

His third knock seemed to set her lips moving. "No," she was saying. "No-no-no-no-no . . . ."

As she spoke, her face retained an uncanny composure, like a death mask. The old man could not tell if she understood she was no longer alone.

The widow continued to disregard him. The old man waited. Then he tried the door.

The glass panel slid aside. He crossed the room, his bare soles indenting the thick, warm pile of the rug. When he stood over the woman, his gaunt shadow seemed to embrace her, but she remained indifferent.

"Myra?"

"No." The word was silent. "No-no-no . . . ."

"Come, Myra."

"No." She continued to keep the sound to herself. "No."

The old man understood perfectly. "No." It was the only answer possible under the circumstances, yet what would be the sense of bringing it out in the open, shouting? This was the sort of restraint the old man comprehended.

He watched the old woman's lips, new to him without their cosmetic crust. Childlike. He wondered if he should slap her . . . gently, the way he had sometimes reclaimed his enchanting child from nightmares. He had held his Deborah, consoling himself for the torment it caused him to slap her. But he could not touch this woman: forgetful of her nakedness, he recalled his own.

"Myra." The old man's voice was abrasive. "Come. Come with me, Myra."

"No. No."

He grasped her elbows and lifted her from the chair. Only her lips put up resistence. "No." Her arms were warmer, more fully fleshed than his. Holding them, he pushed her outside toward his apartment, reliable comfort and safety.

Myra neither fought nor helped him, stumbling the way he steered her, clumsy and malleable as a sleepwalker. The old man grew winded, more from dread than exertion. Then, on the pavement between their two doors, the widow came to a standstill. He could push her no further.

The wind had revived, and when Myra whispered to him, the old man could not make out her words.

"Would you rather I stayed there . . . with you?" he asked.

His certainty slipped. He shouldn't interfere. What was he doing, anyway, leading an unclothed and half-unconscious woman into the dark? What made him think he could look after her? A sense of his own foolishness made him helpless.

As if gauging his weakness, Myra freed herself from his grip and started toward the pool.

"Come back here!" He heard himself: ineffectual, a testy old man who could impose his will on no one, nothing. "Myra!"

The widow did not pause. He had no choice but to go after

her. When he caught her arm again, he felt himself being propelled to the pool's edge. They reached the ladder which dropped into the deepest part of the water. She stopped there, placing both hands on the curved metal handrail, daring the old man to pull her away.

Now, for the first time, she looked at him. Her expression was reasonable and utterly unscrupulous. "I am going to take a swim," she said.

"Myra—,"

"That is what I want to do, Herbert."

"But you can't—."

"I can," she said quietly, stepping out of her slippers.

She let go of the railing. Then, firm and deliberate, Myra Glendenning detached the old man's fingers from her arm and lowered herself down the ladder into the swimming pool.

A cloud like a ruffled curtain slipped from the moon, and a bland face peered down. For a few seconds, the old man stood balanced on the concrete ledge above the naked woman floating in the blue-black pool. His arms were half raised, as if pleading for her return.

"Myra—."

She turned her head away from him and began to swim slowly toward the center of the pool, holding her chin up and moving her arms stiffly. Her skin looked platinum in the moonlight.

Sighing, the old man let his arms drop to his sides. Then he followed her into the warm and inky water, where the wind failed to make itself felt.

Late that night, the old man sat alone in his living room and stared at the telephone. He supposed it was getting near midnight, but he had lost his regard for time. The lamp next to his chair glared in his eyes, and he reached over to turn it off, wincing at a nip of pain in his shoulder. By the dim light from the hallway, he picked up the telephone and dialed.

When she answered, her voice scarcely sounded far away.

"Daughter," he said.

"Daddy?"

"Were you asleep?" The question was without apology.

"What's wrong? Are you all right?"

"I am," he said. "Are you?"

"Sure, but—Daddy, something's the matter. What is it?" She seemed close to tears.

The old man recalled how difficult it had been to convince her of safety when she was small. His child inhabited an unsound world at night. Roused from nightmares, she would make him repeat his assurances a dozen times before she would acquiesce to sleep again. "It was only a dream . . . only a dream," he would tell her. She would make him promise, make him swear, make him cross his heart and hope to die.

He would do all she asked, allowing her little bedside lamp to shine through to dawn, evidence of his good faith. Often he would remain in her room, cramped in the low tufted chair in the corner, staring at the lambs on the pink wallpaper until he fell asleep himself. "You'll spoil her," his wife complained. His comforting became surreptitious.

"It's all right," the old man said now. "Everything is fine, Deborah."

The receiver crackled softly. The old man thought his daughter sighed.

"I wish you would come out here," he said. "For a visit."

"I've got to find a job," Deborah said.

"Can't it wait?"

"I've put it off so long already . . . ."

"You worry too much," the old man said. "I want to see you, Daughter."

She hesitated, and when she replied, he could barely hear her. "You do?"

The doubt and surprise in the question, his daughter's disbelief, brought a shock of pain to the old man. For a moment he could not speak.

"I do," he said at last. "Please."

Deborah was silent, and it occurred to the old man that he might be pressing an unfair advantage, frightening her, catching her off guard.

"If you can," he said. "I'd get your tickets."

"It isn't the money."

"I know," the old man told her. "I know."

He heard her begin to cry.

"It's going to be all right," he said. "Cross my heart."

"I have to learn to look after myself." Her voice was broken.

In that instant, he saw her again: the plain, broad face . . . the gentle mouth, always so uncertain. He wondered where she had come by that terrible uncertainty—surely not from her mother or himself. He listened to her crying and pictured the way her skin would turn angry colors. She was the most enchanting child he had ever seen.

"Look after yourself . . . ," the old man repeated, as if she had said something mysterious. "Yes, I suppose. But not just yet."

"Daddy, I don't know what to do."

"It will be all right," he promised.

"But *how*?"

The old man paused. "I don't know," he said.

In the silence that came across the wire, it seemed to him that he could count each mile that separated him from his child. He thought of the Grand Canyon, the Mississippi River, the Great Lakes. He had failed her.

"Daughter?"

"I'm still here."
"I could come out there. To see you."
"It's winter." Deborah was crying again. "There's snow."
Suddenly, the old man laughed, a low sound from deep within his chest. "You can't scare me," he said.
When he heard the sharp intake of her breath, it suited him to imagine that his daughter was smiling.

Outdoors the wind was battering the date palms again. There was no sound from his bedroom, where the widow slept in his bed, wearing his pajamas, a glass of blackberry brandy on the bedside table. The old man had left a light on for her. He hoped she would not wake and cry in the night. There would be nothing he could do.
Nothing.
He walked to the sofa on fleshless feet, blue with cold. He lay down and covered himself with the gray woolen blanket he had brought with him from New Hampshire. From where he lay, he could see his front door. The hardware, painted to resemble old brass, gleamed dully under the hallway light. The fixtures' false shine offended him. The big square lock, the safety chain, were necessary, he supposed. Permanently affixed. But that flimsy handle—surely he could replace that with a proper doorknob.
He might start scouting around tomorrow, he thought. Take his time. Hold out for exactly what suited him. Perhaps an old-fashioned glass one might turn up somewhere, the kind with facets to reflect the light.
With a fat glass prism revolving slowly behind his eyes, the old man fell asleep. He had forgotten to draw the drapes, and the wind pressed up against his window all night, without breaking or entering his dreams.

BERKIE

Paternity: a word I used lightly, as a younger man. It had to do with disgrace, being hauled into court or bamboozled to the altar, held accountable. Paternity: we joked about it, my friends and I, for it always happened to someone else, some poor fool who didn't know what he was getting into. At eighteen and twenty-two, we were careful: we could afford to smirk.

Later, however, we tossed caution to the winds. Leaving Princeton, we wooed and wed and stalked fortunes. Helped by our newly acquired wives, beautiful young women who burned with wanting, we set small worlds on fire. Paternity: the word vanished from our vocabularies as the condition itself absorbed us. "Janet is pregnant," we said. "Samantha's expecting . . . one on the way." Plainspoken and absurdly proud, we divested fatherhood of its natural terror as blithely as we overlooked the wonder of it. But fathering is an awesome thing, and our first boyish instincts were sound: we should have been afraid.

I stand behind the house at Southhampton, squinting into the piercing light of an October afternoon. We'll close the house for good tomorrow, and when we leave—probably not as early as we mean to, not quite beating the Sunday-night traffic into the city—Janet and I shall put by plans for the winter: skiing in Vermont, a new theatre season, a mid-February week in Aruba or Caneel Bay. Leaving the summer house in late autumn seems the most final of departures. The shutters and storm windows and furniture covers, the bare flagpole at the dock, seem to shut us out of our own life. We never look back as we coast down the driveway, for fear of what might wave from the dark windows. Janet will distract the girls, twelve and eight, with promises: Halloween costumes, ballet lessons, Schrafft's after matinées. Premonition will be preserved in silence. With luck, it will shatter in the burst of another spring.

I scan the lawn that slopes gracefully toward the sea. Twenty-four hours remain, a relatively sure thing. My children play one last game of badminton. Their wiry bodies tensed under bright hooded sweatshirts, they face off like warriors, more silent than I can recall being as a child. But then, as sisters, they play for stakes higher than I, an only child, had to face. My peaceable, indulgent wife and I have bred blood-feud competitors, petite Sabine women with a lust for skirmish and conquest.

Mandy takes a wild, fierce swing. The edge of her racket improbably catches the shuttlecock, sending it in a high arc above the shingled garage. Like a slain bird, it nosedives to the roof and rolls into the gutter.

"Wimp!" Jessica hurls her racket to the ground. The single word hits her younger sister like well-aimed sniper's fire.

"I am not!" Mandy's voice is strangled.

"Big baby. Can't do anything right, you . . . *wimp*." Jessica stalks toward the beach, leaving devastation on the browning grass.

I approach warily. "Bet if you stood on my shoulders you could get it down."

Mandy raises mortally wounded eyes to me. "Daddy, she *always* calls me that."

"What, honey?"

"Wimp."

"Wimp—what's that? Only a word, baby."

"*Oh no it's not!*" Then, her whole frame quivering with outrage, my small daughter enlightens me. She is compelling. By the time she finishes interpreting the insult, revenge appeals to me. I lose myself in one of parenthood's denser mazes: the necessary aloofness from what one's offspring inflict upon each other.

"Never mind," I say.

"But she—."

"I'll tell Jess not to call you that anymore."

"She'll do it when you can't hear."

No doubt she will. My daughters will suffer a host of indignities and griefs which I'll not witness.

I grasp Mandy under the arms and swing her to my shoulder. She might be made of silk and goose down. Not for the first time, I am amazed at the strength I possess when acting as a father, a force I lack as an ordinary man.

My daughter laughs aloud, her sneakers scrambling ruthlessly over tendon and bone to gain a foothold. I sway for an instant beneath her weight, and the tenuous motion delights her. She is impervious to my flesh, my terror under her waffled soles. With appalling disregard, she hurls herself onto the roof and retrieves the shuttlecock.

Poised above me, triumphantly balanced against the brutal blue of sea and sky, my child raises a fistful of white feathers over her head. The fast-sinking sun floods her in an unscrupulous light.

The children are in bed. In the living room, Janet removes cushions from wicker chairs and stuffs them into gleaming black trash bags. I cart the live coals which cooked our dinner to the edge of the beach and bury them in the sand. The grill is still warm when I place it in the garage, among bicycles, croquet and badminton sets, sand chairs, the huge striped umbrella no one but Janet's mother ever uses.

Coming back into the house, I hear radio music from Jessica's room above. My firstborn, growing so tall, so shapely, so secretive. I linger at the foot of the stairs, my hands resting, folded, on the carved oak newel post. Then I climb the stairs, feeling an ache of footprints behind my neck.

"Still awake?"

"Hi, Dad." Jessica turns on the bedside lamp as if she's been expecting me.

"I have something to say to you." I mean to sound stern, or at least solemn, but her tousled hair, her sun-freckled nose, her mother's eyes unman me.

"About Mandy," she says. "I already told her I'm sorry."

"You did?"

She nods, dismissing me. "Dad?"

"Yes, honey?"

"Do you ever think about just staying here all the time?"

She means the place, I know, but when I answer her, I have the time in mind. "Constantly."

"You think we really could?"

I bend to kiss her, tucking her in tight, as I used to do when she was small. "No."

"I didn't think so."

At the doorway, I pause and look back. "Your sister's not a wimp, you know.

Flat on her back, my daughter manages a Gallic shrug, world-weary and wise. Her mind is already on winter.

In the next room, Mandy sleeps. The covers, reaching to her chin, render me useless. No doubt she dreams, the quarrel with her sister forgotten. I alone still feel the sting. Perhaps it is merely seasonal morbidity heightening the seasonless anguish of a father's love, but I can't distinguish it from horror:

This afternoon, in my child's stricken eyes, I encountered Berkie Downes, the ghost of all harm that can come to children. Now, in the dark around my daughter's bed, responsibility looms, monstrous and shadowy. Remembering Berkie, I realize that all my defenses amount to nothing.

"Berkie"—dreadful name for a kid. Berkley Downes, Jr., actually. We lived less than a mile apart, children of privilege in the gracious suburbs north of Chicago, along the lake. Berkie was in my class from the first day of kindergarten until we were seventeen. Had he survived, he too would be over forty now. I cannot imagine him as a man.

Poor Berkie. Memory treats him like a dog. A puny one. Other children would pick him up by the scruff of the neck and drop him. He was a runt, a mutt. At twice his size, I could have lorded it over him. Or run interference for him, I suppose. I did neither. When Berkie's backside was used as a kickball, I tried not to notice. When no one would notice, I tried to be kind. My kindnesses were furtive because I didn't want to be associated with Berkie Downes. His mother, Glynnis, was my mother's best friend. Her son was . . . well, a "wimp."

Mrs. Downes would unburden herself to my mother, who would, in turn, unload on my father. They were acutely aware of Berkie's shortcomings. One person, however, wore that awareness like a hairshirt—Berkie's father, Ziggy. The chafing just about killed him.

Mr. Downes—Berkley, Sr.—got the nickname Ziggy for the way he sliced across the field as an All-American halfback at Purdue. Some Indianapolis sportswriter once referred to him as "Zig-Zag" Downes, and Sigma Chi took it up. Mr. Downes was not, by any stretch of the imagination, a "Berkie."

His boy, however, was. A perfect Berkie. I still recall him, distinct as a photograph, the day we started school: delivered by his mother to the kindergarten playroom, hunkering down in a corner behind a goldfish tank. He doesn't put up much fuss—Berkie was never the tantrum type—but simply crouches there, dripping. He is dressed in short pants and long socks, a blue blazer with no lapels and brass anchors for buttons: a wimp. And he never really changed, even after we got to high school. It was bound to rub a man like Ziggy Downes the wrong way.

I recall, around the sixth grade, coming home from school once and finding Mrs. Downes sitting with my mother in the kitchen breakfast nook drinking tea. I could tell Mrs. Downes had been crying; she quickly turned her face to the latticed ivy wallpaper as I came in.

My mother waved vaguely toward a white waxed-paper bag on the counter. I was fluent in her manual language: "Hi—fresh donuts—get out of here." Mother could demonstrate an admirable economy of expression when she chose. I grabbed two glazed donuts, seeing she was too distracted to make an issue of the second, and got out fast. As I charged up the stairs to change for football, I could hear Berkie's mother:

"You don't know how lucky you are, Jean."

"You mustn't worry so much, Glyn. Berkie will be fine."

Berkie was not fine, of course. He was hopeless. But in those days, people spoke more gently. Berkie was "a problem child." Especially for people like the Downses.

Myopic, disheveled, stunted, athletic nicknames beyond his prospects—Berkie hardly seemed to belong to Ziggy and Glynnis. Which would have been regrettable enough. But he failed on other counts, as well. He was a poor student, and not for lack of effort. He would do his homework, then forget to bring it to class. Or leave it on the bus. Or misunderstand assignments. He was forever reading wrong chapters or violating one-inch margins. The points of his No. 2 pencils would snap sharply during tests, and he would never have a spare. On one occasion, Sister Clothilde, the most patient of women, thundered at him, "Berkley Downes, your penmanship is an abomination!" Sister Clothilde held the Palmer Method nearly as sacred as the Baltimore Catechism. Later, she apologized for her severity, her fat face collapsing in remorse.

"I know you're trying, Berkley," she said.

He was.

Berkie must have been as maladroit at home as he was at school. He broke things. He mumbled when his father fired questions at him. He lost his glasses, fell up and down stairs and from tree-limbs and bicycles. His two younger sisters, Brooke and Belinda, would be dropped at our house for impromptu visits while their brother was rushed to the hospital emergency room. My mother, whose neighborly response to all manner of misfortune was the casserole, stocked the pantry with packaged stroganoff and hollandaise mixes, mushrooms in tins and noodles in cellophane.

When they thought I was out of hearing, my parents made light of the situation. My father called Berkie "Calamity James." Beneath the banter, however, I sensed genuine sympathy for the Downeses. Berkie was a commonly held sorrow which bound our two families together.

Berkie was something of a problem for me, too. Of course, it wasn't my Baccarat stemware he shattered, my college yearbook he doused in Dr. Pepper. I never had to stand in hospital hallways attending the setting of his bones and the stitching of his skin, nor concern myself with ruinous penmanship, casseroles, child minding. I did, however, share some of the adults' burden. Berkie's gentle ineptitude posed a moral dilemma for all of us:

Berkie Downes tried the collective patience; he tested to its limits the individual soul. He riled tempers, drawing to himself chastening outbursts of intolerance. But worst of all, although Berkie was goodness itself, he was an embarrassment. Our embarrassment reproached and reduced us.

My adolescent conscience dropped occasional hints to me about solace, rescue, reform. Absorbed by my own growing pains, I turned them aside.

The bind Berkie put me in eased considerably after grammar school. The public high school we attended was immense—nearly eight hundred in our class alone. Berkie got lost in the shuffle quickly and easily.

The first two years, we met only in passing; we had none of

the same classes. I had advanced to the front: "Curriculum–Accelerated." Berkie brought up the rear: "Remedial–Special Attention."

In the afternoons after school, I migrated like a predatory bird to the green metal locker rooms, the green-tiled showers, the green playing fields. I was on the Junior Varsity teams in both football and baseball. Off-season, I worked out with weights, did the requisite studying, and kept an eye on Marietta Tandy, a girl from my biology class who had a precocious chest, a dreamer's gaze, and an A-minus average. Marietta lived in a splendid Tudor house in Kenilworth. Her next-door neighbor, Todd Mathison, played JV baseball with me, and I actively cultivated him, spending more time at his house than my own. Where Berkie went after school was a mystery I never pondered. Maybe he just went home and knocked things over.

My parents were seeing less of the Downeses by this time. Mr. Downes was running to fat, drinking more than my parents found acceptable. Although Saturday night foursomes at the country club were less frequent than they once had been, Mrs. Downes continued to drop by on weekday afternoons. She often looked puffy around the eyes, but she was beautiful even then.

Glynnis Downes came from California. She wore vivid colors like pink and green at the same time, and tied her pale hair in a ponytail, except when she dressed up. Then she would pile her hair high, wearing swishy black dresses and spike heels. In the afternoons, though, she had on flat-heeled pastel shoes like a ballerina's slippers. I was getting tall, and I felt like Superman when I stood anywhere near her.

My mother said Mrs. Downes was once a princess in the Rose Parade in Pasadena, that she barely missed being queen. You might have guessed it, just to look at her. Except it was hard to believe she'd come in second. I realize, now, how much

Berkie resembled her: small and gentle, a bruised look to the wide gray eyes. Over the high whistle of the tea kettle, my mother's low voice, "Now, Glyn . . . ," didn't tell me much. But enough. Ziggy was getting worse, and Berkie wasn't getting any better.

Ziggy Downes was a big, boistrous man, the only friend of my parents who never bothered to lower his voice on the punchlines of dirty jokes. The jokes were not really out of line, just what they used to call "off-color." And Ziggy was a very good storyteller. He paid a lot of attention to me, giving me rabbit punches, calling me a chip off the old block. Since my father stuck to golf, tennis, and handball, I wasn't sure just which block Ziggy meant.

The Downeses lived in an imposing brick house on the perimeter of the Glenhollow Golf Course. It must have been built back in the '20s, before the Depression turned servants' quarters into an anachronism. A buzzer was imbedded in the floor under the dining room table; it sounded imperiously whenever Jeeves, the Downeses' English bulldog, stumbled upon it with one of his great paws.

Glynnis Downes airily mocked the house's grandeur. She loved having company, but she cooked and served the meals herself. The clothes she wore for such occasions were like costumes—caftans, embroidered peasant blouses, toreador pants with spangled vests. She usually seated us children at the table with the adults, but she refused to cater to our pedestrian tastes. We were force-fed grown-up delicacies like shad roe and chutney. Sitting on a telephone book at Glynnis's table, I received my first instruction in dissecting an artichoke. I can still picture her quick, suntanned hands, opals glowing on two fingers, as she peeled away the fine inner thorns and sliced the heart for me.

One would think I might have noticed that the Downeses

had money, that in fact they were enormously rich. But I gave no thought to wealth. Nearly everybody on the North Shore had it, or seemed to. The Downeses were like everyone else in Winnetka, aside from the random nuance—a Californian eye for color, a trophy case in the den, a son who was a wimp. Like most children, I possessed a savage disregard for detail.

My father told me later—in the course of some object-lesson on values, I believe—that Ziggy Downes had inherited his business from his father, a large concern which manufactured industrial safety devices. Ziggy was president and principal stockholder of the firm, but apparently commerce never captivated him as football had. Perhaps the competition wasn't strong enough. In any case, according to my father, life was all downhill for Ziggy after gridiron season.

Idle hands, idle riches, idle speculation aside, though, it did seem a cruel twist for the football hero to lack an heir to his interests. Perhaps in its way, life had been as ungenerous to father as to son.

From what Glynnis told my mother, Berkie's fortunes declined drastically at puberty, when a no-holds-barred battle erupted with poor Berkie as the disputed territory. Presumably without malice, but certainly without much restraint, Ziggy mapped out a rite of passage to instill in his son the qualities of an All-American: strength and stamina. No kid of his was a born loser—he'd see to that.

In a blitzkrieg of fatherly attention, Berkie Downes was acquainted with his deficiencies and reminded of his failures. He was interrogated at meals, accused at bedtime. His posture and diction were mercilessly corrected. Instructed to catch his father's bullet-like passes on the back lawn, he was made to miss them by—what? Poor eyesight, slow feet, clumsy hands, a dysfunctional killer-instinct? Cause scarcely matters. Berkie missed his father's passes by a mile.

As often happens with open declarations of war, the battle over Berkie's well-being was escalated by alliance and entanglement. Glynnis, her weeping previously confined to the no-man's-land of my mother's kitchen, entered the fray. She was determined to protect her son, or at the very least to console him. Her involvement proved disastrous. Ziggy, staunch believer in brute force, redoubled his efforts and his son's misery. His wife's frail defenses crumbled. Teachers of the two younger children expressed concern over one's misbehavior, the other's listlessness. The Downeses were not holding their own.

My awareness of the hostilities was marginal. I knew Mrs. Downes came over more frequently in the afternoons. I picked up the sympathy in my mother's murmuring. Otherwise, I was as impervious to the Downeses' disintegration as I had been, all along, to Berkie.

In junior year, Berkie and I were capriciously flung together by locker assignments. I bumped into him, more than figuratively, on the first day of school, flattening him against a row of tinny doors as I sped around a corner. The top of Berkie's head came not quite to my shoulder, and I had knocked his glasses askew with my physics book. He seemed to look up at me with three eyes.

"Berkie!" I grasped his elbow and hauled him from a gaping locker.

"Hey, Josh." Although the fault was clearly mine, his smile was automatically apologetic.

"You okay?"

He looked awful. His face was sunburned and peeling, yet there was a grayish cast to his complexion. I had been at a football camp in Wisconsin for most of the summer, so I hadn't seen Berkie. He had lost weight since June. Bluish veins stood out in his neck. Even his dull, ash-colored hair looked thinner: when he bent to pick up his gym bag, I saw raw-looking patches of scalp on the crown of his head.

"Sure. Fine." He crouched over the red canvas bag, his reply addressed to my knees. "Your locker must be around here, too, Josh. I saw your name near mine on the list in the office."

Like everything else about him, Berkie's conversation was clumsy and slow. His awkwardness seemed contagious: I always had trouble thinking what to say to him.

"So . . . how was your summer, Berk?"

"Okay," he said. "Yours?"

"Great. I was up in Madison—."

"Yeah. My Dad told me."

Mr. Downes had been waiting at our house the night I got home from camp, avid to hear about new plays, Wisconsin's likely starting line-up. He had taken to calling me "sport" and forcing me to spar with him, a ritual which brought a look of irritation to my father's normally placid face.

"So how was it?" Berkie asked.

"Great. Terrific."

Berkie glanced away with an enigmatic smile. "Great game, football."

"Hey, listen . . . what have you been up to, anyway?"

He shrugged, fiddling with the zipper of his gym bag. He had straightened up again, standing on one leg with the bag propped on his raised knee. The lace of a sneaker was jamming the zipper. "The yard," he mumbled, working the lace more firmly into the zipper's teeth.

"What?"

Berkie lost his balance and started to tumble against me. Then he caught himself. "I did the yard. See you, Josh."

Still worrying the zipper, a vague, misaligned grin on his face, Berkie shambled down the corridor. His narrow shoulders were hunched, ready for the next assault.

This odd conversation with Berkie only made sense later, when my parents mentioned the Downeses' gardener being let go. A summer of outdoor work, Ziggy had announced, would be just the thing to toughen the kid up. Glynnis's protests had been useless. Whenever Ziggy went down to the Loop to look in on the business, she and the little girls surreptitiously helped with the weeding. Otherwise, there was little she could do.

The Downes place had about five acres of lawn, flower beds and rock gardens, a vegetable patch, a pool, and a small greenhouse. Throughout the summer, Berkie had grappled with the growing season from dawn to dusk. His only respite came by way of sessions with a remedial reading specialist three afternoons a week. Glynnis told my mother, with a tearful laugh, that it took Berkie all of July and August to get through *Billy Budd* and the grounds looked like they'd been tended by a finicky goat.

With adjoining lockers, Berkie and I saw each other several times a day. We always said hello, rarely more than that. From what I could see, he was even less talkative with everyone else.

I wonder, now, if he wanted a friend. If he carried a visible sorrow on his slight frame and I just missed it. But even now, I recall him with an easy smile, the look of someone telling himself jokes. It was as if he had inherited his father's relish for punchlines and simply lacked the talent for delivery.

One October day our paths intersected when there were no witnesses. It was lunch period, and the high school corridors were empty. Returning to my locker to pick up a forgotten calculus book, I found Berkie on a marble ledge, nestled in a window's frame like an off-center gargoyle.

"Hey," he said.
"What are you doing, Berkie?"
"Nothing."
He looked more amused than usual. His nose was still peeling, and he wore a misshapen brown sweater with a herd of harnessed reindeer prancing across his chest. I couldn't believe his mother would let him out of the house in that sweater.
"Aren't you having lunch?"
Berkie shrugged. "I forgot my money."
For some reason, his diffidence suddenly infuriated me. "Jesus Christ!" I felt like taking a punch at him.
Berkie lowered his chin to one corduroy knee. "I'm quite a problem," he said agreeably.
Then he smiled, actually smug: a punchline. His delivery was flawless.
Caught by surprise, I whooped. My laugh reverberated wildly in the deserted hallway. A janitor peered out from a supply closet, suspicion visible on his face at fifty yards.
"Come on, kid. I've got some money. I'll buy you lunch."
Berkie studied the floor. "Naw."
"Come on." I grabbed him by the scruff of the neck and tipped him off the windowsill, clutching Donner and Blitzen until he gained his footing.
"You don't have to—."
"Look, Berk, we've known each other since we were five and I've never taken you to lunch, right?"
"Yeah, well . . . ."
"I'm a sentimental guy, see?" I pulled his sweater behind me toward the cafeteria.
"I'll pay you back, Josh."
His lunch came to twenty-five cents: a dime bag of caramel corn, chocolate milk, and a dish of stewed prunes. I looked at his tray and thought what I had known all along: the kid really was hopeless.

BERKIE

The cafeteria was crowded, but we found an empty table near the corner where the teachers usually sat. Berkie had finished the prunes and was working on the chocolate milk when he started talking. "You hear about next weekend?"
"No, what?"
His expression brightened, and he set down his milk carton. "My Dad's taking me up north, just the two of us. We got sleeping bags and—."
I looked over my shoulder to see what was stopping him cold: Marietta coming toward us in a white angora sweater.
"Listen, I gotta go." Berkie tried to sound like he'd just remembered something important. His face was red, and he nearly tipped his chair backward getting up.
"Berk, hold on a second—."
He didn't seem to hear me. He grabbed the bag of caramel corn. Then he was cutting in and out of the crowd, finding small openings to squeeze through, and he was gone.
Marietta gave me a curious look. "Who's the gnome?"
"Forget it."
"Who *is* he, Josh?"
"Ah, nobody . . . just a friend of the family."

I largely forgot that lunch with Berkie until a couple of weeks later. My parents, thinking I'd gone up to study, were talking one night after dinner. They were discussing the Downeses—I could tell that much, but I wasn't especially interested.
"What *can* he be thinking of?" my mother said. "Inexcusable . . . ." As the note of trouble in her voice relayed itself to me, I stopped flipping the pages of *Sports Illustrated.*
"Now, Jean, remember you've only heard *her* side."
"True. But you know Ziggy . . . and Berkie's so . . . ."
"Berkie." Autumn rain dashed against the window like static. ". . . hunting . . . ." I heard. ". . . senseless . . . ."
"I'm inclined to agree, certainly," my father said. "But not

161

everyone feels as we do. Besides, you'll admit his concern for the boy is justified. I'm sure he thinks he's doing what's . . . ."

Like many well-bred women, my mother was trained to drop her voice when agitated. My ear picked up a scramble of consonants without vowels. I heard a word that sounded like "gun."

"Perhaps not to *my* taste, but a perfectly respectable sport . . . ."

"For a sensitive child? So frail . . . shoulder black and blue, Glyn said . . . ."

"Those rifles have a kick."

"I'm not interested in the technicalities, Charlie . . . sheer cruelty . . . knows how the boys loves animals, how gentle . . . to make him dress the deer . . . still vomiting when they got . . . ."

"It does seem excessive, I'll grant you."

Mother was growing restive under my father's unremitting fairness. "Criminal," she said.

The charge might have been raised against my father, as well as Ziggy Downes. In some way, I felt it applied to me, too.

"Children." My father's voice sounded both wistful and angry. "Who ever knows what's best?"

Fathers were supposed to, in those days. I climbed the stairs, silent as a cat burglar, and shut the door to my room, closing the Downeses and their troubles inside with me. Berkie was beginning to get on my nerves.

I didn't meet Berkie again until the following week, on Monday morning. From down the hall, I observed him kicking his locker door. He perpetrated the small violence as if his heart wasn't in it. The latch was stuck, and I helped him loosen it. His fingers trembled as he turned the combination lock, and

BERKIE

there was dirt under his nails, even though they were bitten nearly to the quick.

"Been sick, Berkie? I haven't seen you."

"Yeah."

"You okay now?"

"Yeah."

Berkie turned and walked off, his eyes blank. His khaki pants, grass-stained on the seat, were too large, bunched at the waist with a childish cowboy belt studded with colored glass stars.

He hadn't shut his locker. I did it hesitantly, wondering whether he would be able to open it later. The trivial gesture made me feel responsible for him.

But the next morning, Berkie seemed to have things under control when I found him hovering in front of my locker. His books were piled under one arm, and he extended his free hand, palm up, toward me. The smile on his skinny, pale face was pure and almost brilliant. Sunlight refracting from his glasses opaqued his eyes. His clothes fit properly, no infantile design on his navy sweater, no cowboy belt. He had a certain dignity, and I wondered for a second if Berkie might have found himself a girl.

"Hey," he said.

"Hey, Berkie." I indicated the quarter in his open palm. "What's this?"

"For lunch."

"I said I was buying."

"And I said I'd pay you back."

"Listen, I—."

"Take it," he said. "Thanks for fixing my locker, too."

"Sure, but—."

His smile grew strained. "Take the money. Please, Josh."

I shrugged and let Berkie drop the quarter into my hand. It was sweaty.

"Thanks," he said.

I grinned. "Let's do it again sometime."

For an instant, Berkie seemed confused. The expression on his face reminded me of the hunting trip. His eyes looked frantic with indecision, like the eyes of an animal trapped in headlights.

Then he moved away. "Yeah, sure," he said. "See you, Josh."

I stood watching Berkie fight his way down the hall until the crowd swallowed him whole.

That afternoon, the Varsity scrimmaged the JVs after school. Coach Greenough gave me a lot of play, and I spotted Marietta in the stands, her gold sweater and hair catching the waning light. Whenever I made a good play, I was sure I could hear her cheer above the others.

We stopped in High's Variety for cokes after the scrimmage, so it was nearly six-thirty by the time I was arriving home. I was whistling something romantic and jaunty as I rounded the corner of our street.

Our house stood out, shimmering, from a block away. Every light was on, even in the vacant garage, whose automatic doors were up, exposing my father's orderly arrangement of rakes and power tools and lawn games. The sight seemed slightly untoward, a domestic intimacy displayed to the neighborhood. For a second, I slowed down, staring at my own house as if I had never seen it before. Then I began to run.

The front door was unlocked. There was no note on the table in the entry hall. No message by the kitchen phone. A roast was thawing on the drainboard, its pale red juices trickling into the white porcelain sink.

"Hello?" I called.

No one answered.

The table had not been set for dinner. There were no aromas of cooking food, and the oven door was cold when I placed my hand on it. I felt a dizzying alarm. In a household as orderly, punctual, and habit-bound as ours, deviation in routine suggested calamity.

I flinched at the piercing sound of the telephone, but reached it before the second ring.

"Josh?" My mother's voice was low, yet taut as the overtightened strings of some delicate musical instrument. "Son?"

"Mom, where *are* you?"

"Were you worried?" I could barely hear her. "Dad and I are fine, Josh. We're at the Downeses'. Your father will be right home . . . wait for him, Josh."

"Mom?"

"Wait, son." The connection was broken.

My mother rarely used my name, and she never called me "son." Most often she called me "dear," as if she didn't quite trust herself to distinguish me from my father.

Ten minutes later, the Lincoln coasted into the garage, but my father didn't come immediately into the house. I already had one hand on the door when I felt him pushing it from the other side.

It seemed that my father's worn, familiar face had been redesigned. It looked pitted, hallowed, and abandoned, like an ancient burial ground.

"Dad, what is it?"

"There's been an accident, Josh." He spoke slowly, as if taking great pains with me. "At the Downeses'."

"Berkie—?" I couldn't imagine an accident befalling anyone else.

"Berkie." My father, a spare man, let his weight fall to a kitchen chair so hard that I heard wood crack, a sound like the breaking of bone.

"What happened? Is he going to be—?"

The flat of his hand slammed down on the tabletop, making the sugar bowl jump. "No!" he shouted. "Berkie is *not* going to be all right."

I stared. His anger was so unexpected that his meaning nearly escaped me.

"*Berkie Downes is not going to be all right!*"

Then the fury went out of him. He lowered his head, resting it on his folded arms, and cried. He sounded as if he had never quite learned how, had not supposed he would need to. The grating of my father's unaccustomed grief made me suddenly aware how little protection this world will promise a man.

Berkie was dead. I knew that. But I didn't know how or why. I stood with my back to my father and stared at the blood which had seeped from the meat to the perforated metal disc that covered the drain, delicate red arteries like rivers on a map. My hands were cold. I put them in my pockets, feeling the warm coins there, wondering if I still had Berkie's quarter.

"He was all right this morning." I turned and took two steps toward my father, then hesitated.

His voice was muffled in the sleeve of his raincoat. "Berkie was never all right."

I went to him, reaching out to touch his back between the shoulder blades.

After a moment, my father lifted his head and looked at me, hard, as if he suspected me of withholding a terrible secret from him. "You wouldn't think a man could fail to see something so plain, would you?"

He was not talking to me.

I didn't learn what had actually happened until my mother came home. By that time, I felt I'd already heard the story a dozen times.

Berkie Downes had left school in the late morning, returning to an empty house. In the kitchen he opened a bottle of Dr.Pepper, but he didn't drink it. Sometime before one-thirty, he went to the den and removed one of his father's rifles from an antique glass and mahogany cabinet. He carried the gun upstairs and, standing in the shower stall of his parents' white marble bathroom, Berkie fired a single shot into his left temple.

Glynnis Downes discovered her son's body when she came home from her tennis lesson. There was no note, and relatively little mess.

Berkie had been careful.

Berkley Downes, Jr., was buried on a Friday, after a Requiem Mass at Saint Francis of Assisi Church. The service was conducted by a young, rather vague priest, new to the parish. He mentioned Berkie's "illness," and quoted from the New Testament: "Suffer little children to come unto Me."

Although it was late autumn, the day was fine and warm. Glynnis Downes, wearing one of her swishy black dresses but not spike heeled shoes, looked insubstantial beside her husband. Her hair fell loose to her shoulders beneath a Spanish lace mantilla. When the bronze casket was lowered into the ground, Glynnis and Ziggy leaned slightly against one another, staring at the mangled earth with dry, blank eyes. Their daughters, too young to understand, huddled together at the edge of their brother's grave, looking lost.

After the burial, relatives and a few close friends of the family were invited to the Downeses' for lunch. Maids in black uniforms and crisp white aprons passed small glasses of wine and avocado finger-sandwiches on earth-colored platters. On a sideboard, below a Munch drawing of a screaming woman, the cakes and fruits and cheeses were scarcely touched. I remember my mother and Glynnis, two slender women in black, still young, sitting on the piano bench in the corner, behind a Steinway baby grand. Their shoulders were touching. I looked away for a moment. When I turned around again, they were gone.

In midafternoon, as people were beginning to leave, my mother came down the wide, curved stairway as far as the landing. I was leaning against the bannister below, itchy in my wool suit, while Mr. Downes and Berkie's uncle from Santa Barbara advised me about football scholarships. Ziggy was quietly drunk.

"Josh," my mother called softly.

The two men continued talking, seeming not to notice as I was called upstairs.

"She wants to see you for a moment."

Glynnis Downes was sitting at the foot of a satin-covered chaise longue in a beige and salmon bedroom filled with flowers. She still wore her severe dress, but her feet were bare and her hair was fastened in back by an oval tortoise-shell comb. Her face reddened with weeping and cold water, she looked like an exhausted child, roused abruptly from a nap. She smiled at me.

My mother left us, shutting the door, and Glynnis patted a place beside her on the chaise. I took it awkwardly. I don't know what I expected her to say, but I was frightened. Of failing her, perhaps.

"I'm sorry," I said.

"I know, Josh . . . this is so hard . . . especially at your age." Her voice caught, and I waited for her to weep, but she didn't. In fact, a slight smile continued to linger around her mouth. The resemblance to her son was unmistakable.

"Berkie didn't have many friends," she said.

"Oh, that's not—."

"It's all right, Josh. He was . . . an unusual boy."

I lowered my head.

"Josh?"
She was asking that I look at her. I did.
"You were always good to him . . . I noticed that."
I stared into her eyes, forbidding myself to glance away.
"Good to him," she repeated.
At last I saw the one thing I could do. "Berkie and I . . . we were friends," I told her.
Glynnis raised her chin and kissed me on the forehead. Her hair smelled like a summer garden.
"Yes," she said. "Friends."

In the months that followed, the Downeses lived with their grief as best they could, behaving as one might have expected. If Ziggy drank a bit more, if Glynnis cried a bit more, certainly nobody blamed them. In June their lawn looked like a velvet comforter spread out in the sun, and flowers banked the long driveway. At the end of the summer, the year after Berkie died, the house near the country club was sold to a young couple from the city. We heard the wife was a niece of Marshall Field.

The Downeses moved to Tucson, and we did not see them again. But Glynnis and my mother kept in touch. Every Christmas for twenty years my mother would read me the note on a Christmas card from Glynnis Downes. She always mentioned Berkie. And me. And how we were friends from the very first day of kindergarten.

Berkie Downes died twenty-five years ago, and I am still asking why. Mistakes, oversights, miscalculations . . . all fathers make them, but not all children survive them. You do the best you can . . . try to be a good son, hoping for a parity in that which might help you to be a good father. But as my own father said, who ever knows what's best?

Soon my daughters will be too old, too distant, for me to

keep them in sight. My Jessica and Mandy . . . I study them now, taking advantage of the lull. I search for signs of sorrow concealed in their frail limbs and shiny hair, their chapped lips and wise, spooky eyes. Yet even if I should discover such signs, who's to say I'd know what to do?

A quarter of a century intervenes now between Berkie Downes and myself. He remains a child; I have become a father. How can it be that I know so much less now . . . less than I knew at seventeen . . . less than I meant to know by this time? Perhaps it's the disregard for detail which lends the young their certainties. If only those certainties did not have to predecease us.

Paternity: a blind groping of the soul, not much different, no more sure, than the witlessly hopeful travel of sperm. Our conceptions are always accidental, in a sense. And if we knew the odds against them, knew what we'd be getting into . . . .

How does a man come by the bravado for fathering? I do not know. It gives me something to think about, though, these nights I stand watch over my children, a sentry on the lookout for a hint of furtive sorrow.

BROWSING

BROWSING

I see my ex-husband at a yard sale.
Immediately I duck behind a metal utility cabinet, which has been painted green and decorated with vegetable decals. A moment ago, I was browsing, a decent pursuit. Now I am lurking. Craven.
It is not that I mind seeing him. On the contrary, my instinctive self-concealment is in concert with that very desire: I *want* to see my ex-husband. To observe him. How does he conduct himself, alone, on a Saturday morning, at a sale of second-hand goods? What is he in the market for? In calculating the long division of our property, did I manage to cancel out some object, functional or ornamental, that he finds he can't live without? Perhaps I should have consulted him about the garlic press, ask if he wanted a divider for the top kitchen drawer. Who am I, after all, to presume he would eat in restaurants all the time, that the sight of his few forks lying in a jumble with his knives and spoons would not pain him? It is possible that he may turn out to be a better cook than I am. After all, I know so little about him.
He moves closer to me. The utility cabinet is too narrow. It is only a matter of time before I am discovered: lurking. He is taller than I remember. Still a growing boy, perhaps? He bends over, nearly halving himself, to scrutinize a table of kitchen gadgets and curios dispossessed of their cabinets. Yes, the garlic press, I think, guilty as sin over the scampi and salad dressings I've prepared and consumed with splendid disregard for the wants of my one-time spouse. The egg timer. Two wire whisks. I had no shame. That is not the case now.
Gregory, assuming that is still his name (his name—oh God, I even kept half of that), is arrested by something on the table. He freezes in a half-crouch, his face as respectfully bemused as an anthropologist confronted with some aboriginal artifact of worship or war. He makes no attempt to mask his ignorance,

173

but is careful not to give offense. His long-fingered, white, shockingly beautiful hand reaches for something with prudent reverence. He straightens his spine as he lifts it: a pronged wooden mallet. He examines the object at not quite arm's length, his eyes vaguely shocked. Little as I know him, I know he is imagining domestic violence.

"It's for spaghetti," I say, stepping out from behind the green metal sarcophagus, animated as its brash border of peppers and radishes.

"Hello, Ruth."

It is like old times. I never was able to catch him offguard.

"I haven't got one myself, but you sort of wind the strands around those little spikes to lift them out of the boiling water. I think that's the idea."

Gregory nods politely. I am the aborigine, bellicose and goddazed. My former spouse is a respecter of alien and primitive cultures. He sets the wooden mallet back on the table, just where it was, between a food scale and a calico woman with yarn hair who hides a roll of toilet paper under her skirts.

"How are you?" he asks me. I recall the grounds for our divorce: irreconcilable courtesy. He started it. I retaliated, viciously civil.

"It isn't so bad," I say. "Really not so bad."

"No, it isn't, is it?"

"You look good. Better, I mean. Not so thin."

"I don't get enough exercise."

"I meant it as a compliment," I tell him.

"I know you did."

His fine, flyaway hair, unduly red on a man nearing forty, needs cutting. It curls over the back of his collar so I can't tell if his pink oxford cloth shirt is clean and in good repair. I find no fault with the front. No buttons appear to be missing. But then, finding fault with Gregory was never easy.

"You're on sabbatical this semester?"

His light gray eyes blink once behind the polished lenses of his rimless glasses, as if I've reminded him of something he'd prefer to overlook. "Yes. Working full-time on the book."

The book: "Love's Iconoclast: The Demystification of Romance in the Novels of D. H. Lawrence." Only a working title, but how could I compete with that?

"It must be a relief—being able to concentrate on it, I mean."

The iconoclast smiles. "Actually, it means there's no relief. No excuse not to finish now."

"You'll do it." Finish, or find an excuse? I leave the choice of my meaning up to him.

He ignores my ambiguity, a characteristic failing. "What about you—are you doing anything now?"

"By *your* standards, you mean?"

"Oh, Ruth . . . ."

"Sorry. I'm still a sucker for a straight line."

"I wish we could be friends. I'd like this to be . . . amicable."

"It never really was. Maybe you wouldn't take things so hard if you remembered that."

I pick up a set of steak knives with pistol-shaped handles. There are five, bound together with a greasy leather thong. I take care to hold the points in a neutral direction. My ex-husband is shaking his head sadly. "Do you have any steak knives?"

"I don't eat at home much," he says.

"Then you have everything you need."

He shrugs, smiling in a way I find new and attractive. He has learned a thing or two about irony.

"Ask me again," I say.

"What?"

"If I'm doing anything."

His innocent face ages abruptly with wariness. He takes his time, thinking the semantic problem through. "What are you doing now?"

I reward him with what may be my last ingenuous smile, preserved from my girlhood for just such a moment. "I've applied to law school. Finally."

He straightens his shoulders, as if a burden has been shifted to someone else. "I always knew you would." When he reaches toward me to remove the steak knives from my hands, his cool, pale fingers brush my knuckles. "I'm glad for you."

"I haven't been accepted yet."

"*Pro forma*," he says. "Nothing to it."

Self-conscious, I study the display of linens hanging on a clothesline behind him: assorted napkins and tea towels, dresser scarves and doilies. Irish linen, Belgian lace, unbleached muslin cross-stitched and appliquéd by hand. That sort of fancywork isn't done anymore. I knitted a sweater for Gregory while he was writing his dissertation. The sleeves were too short. I sometimes wore it to bed during the winter, when we lived in a basement apartment in Morningside Heights. We have come up in the world: a yard sale in Amherst. Evidently we are both still in the market for something. A bargain. A finishing touch.

"I didn't do badly on the LSATs."

"I'm not surprised. You're going to make one hell of a lawyer."

"Maybe . . . if I meet one."

His laugh exists for the sole purpose of humoring me. It costs him. "I'm still your straight man," he says, believing it.

"And I'm still your friend," I lie.

"Prove it." This time he does not smile.

"What?"

"Let me get you a present, Ruth."

"I don't . . . ."
He stands his ground. "Treasure hunt," he says.

The first year we were married, a ritual more passionate and tender than newlywed lovemaking: the last Saturday of each month, scraping bottom, waiting for the next fellowship check, the thin salary envelope from the Institute for Global Concerns, where I typed position papers that didn't concern me . . . .

The first year of marriage, the last Saturday of the month, my young husband and I would take our bottom dollars—one for each of us—and go off to buy one another gifts.

We would comb the Salvation Army stores, flea markets, junk shops, craft fairs in the parks. Hunting. I recall the treasures we turned up more clearly than the opulent wedding gifts from family friends. The life we made was never suited to silver trays and chafing dishes. Crystal goblets seemed to sour what wine we could afford. When candles burned in our cramped apartments, it seemed simpler to blow them out than to find the sterling snuffer, a gracefully inverted bell on a wand-like handle.

I wore the colored glass earrings my husband pulled from his pockets, though. Even now I have the potholder from the St. Louis World's Fair in my latest kitchen, a bookmark made from a laminated scrap of an old quilt, three wooden buttons from Africa in the shape of elephants' heads, a mauve feather boa that sheds, and a small glass ashtray—"Souvenir of Shreveport, La. Hot Sauce Capital of the World."

And Gregory—do you still, when occasion demands it, work your heels into your dress shoes with the ivory-colored plastic shoehorn endorsing Aldo R. Bianchi for Judge of Probate? Still open beer cans with a lurid naked lady who has a church-key for a head? Do you thumb a long-outdated edition of Guinness's records now and then, seeking food for thought?

I do not imagine my former husband recalls the circle pin enameled with flowers. I wore it on my bathing suit all summer, the year we lived near Crane's Beach. The salt water wore the flowers away, and in September, when school was starting someplace else, even the metal was corroding. Gregory would have no way of knowing, now, that I finally found a chenille bed jacket. The other day I removed three pearly blue discs from it, replacing them with the heads of small elephants who keep their trunks folded under, where they cannot catch on anything. I always used what he gave me . . . eventually.

"Treasure hunt?" I echo my ex-husband faintly, as if he has proposed a suicide pact. He stares into my eyes, challenging my well-known penchant for gracious acquiescence. He knows my greatest weakness: I am a good sport.

"The limits?"

He looks at his wrist watch. "Ten minutes," he says. "One dollar."

I scan the yard sale quickly. I haven't foraged much these past few years. I am rusty. My eye isn't as sharp as it used to be. "Fifteen," I counter. "Two dollars."

In the end we compromise: a quarter of an hour, a dollar and a half.

By custom old enough to have become instinct, we turn and move off in opposite directions. The rules need no elaborating. We'll meet at the appointed time on the spot where we parted. We have learned how to avoid each other in crowds. I cheat and look back: Gregory is bent low over a display of Avon bottles and campaign buttons. He is only warming up. We both know he won't capture my essence among perfumes and politics.

When we played before, in our heyday ten years ago, he invariably won. His gift was always better for me than mine was for him. The intervening years have taught me something: he has me at a perpetual disadvantage. I have never known the opposition as well as I should.

The pressure is on. This is my last chance. A gift, both parties concur, is a statement. It is better, safer, to give than to receive. But from either position, misstep can be lethal.

I am trapped. This Saturday morning, I came without guile to survey my neighbor's goods. I didn't expect to covet them, and I don't. Just looking. I am in the market for something, it's true, but I'm not sure I'd know it if I saw it. Or that I could afford it. If there's one thing I don't need, though, it's gadgetry. Memorabilia. Running into my ex-husband and playing games.

But here we are. Opportunity knocks. I believe, even now, in grace under pressure, fate, good things in small packages, and summing up. This is probably the last possible moment for my parting shot. I can tell the red-haired stranger I was married to just exactly what I think of him now—that is, I could if I knew.

Longingly, I reconsider the steak knives, attracted by their easy suitability. Sharp serrated blades, grips like dueling pistols. The gauntlet has been thrown down; I have no second, and the choice of weapons was not mine. Appropriate in the extreme, those knives. But they cost five dollars, and I would not let him catch me in a deception at the last minute. I wonder if I might find the owner of this yard, these goods, plead a case for being allowed to purchase a single utensil? I'd gladly pay a dollar, as high as a dollar-fifty, for the privilege of taking away the odd one, breaking up the already-broken set.

But I put the knives back where they belong. I knew all along, really, that their symbolism was too facile. Heavy-handed. Not the last impression I'd care to make.

I stand, irresolute, among the tables and cartons of a household's offal. Time is running short. Nearby, a woman with a fraying chiffon scarf tied over her gray hair sits in a canvas director's chair. Her attitude is proprietary. I glance rather desperately at her. "Looking for anything in particular?" she wants to know, in the voice of one who has every right to ask.

"Not exactly, but . . . you wouldn't have a garlic press, would you?"

"Wait," she says.

Wobbling on swollen ankles and perversely high-heeled shoes, she goes to a nearby table, rummages through several small boxes. When she turns around, her expression is arrogant with triumph. She raises the tarnished metal tool over her head so I can see it, a prize.

"How much?" I ask her.

"Guess you could have it for a dollar."

I take it from her without examining the merchandise. I dig out a wallet from my shoulder bag and remove six quarters, put by for the laundromat. "A little extra for your trouble," I say, turning away quickly so I won't have to confront her suspicions.

I return just under the wire. Gregory is already standing where I left him, holding a rumpled brown grocery bag in his arms like a baby. From ten yards away, I can see he has chalked up another victory. It will, I believe, be his last. As I reach him, I take the garlic press from my purse and hand it to him. The pleasure is all mine: replacing one of the many things he has no idea I took from him.

He does not know what it is. That is hardly my concern. He'll have to find out for himself. "Very nice," he says, guarded. No doubt he is imagining his thumb, grasped in the blunt metal vice. Minced: one of many terms unfamiliar to him. He will learn.

Slowly my ex-husband reaches inside the paper bag and pulls out a plaster of Paris statue. Once painted to resemble bronze, it is a woman, seated on a pedestal. Draped rather sloppily in a loose garment, its folds forever stiff, she wears a blindfold and holds a set of scales in one hand.

"Justice," I whisper, awed by his effrontery.

"*Amicus curiae*," says my former husband, establishing his innocence once and for all.

Justice is a lady. I touch her face, where the nose has chipped away to show white. I do not allude to her blindfold, nor the fact that the scales seem askance. This is easier than I anticipated, accepting a parting gift from my ex-husband. He doesn't know what I like anymore.

"*Amicus*," I say, putting the sightless, battered woman back in her bag and preparing to move on. The next time I'm in a mood to shop around, I'll think twice about where I go browsing. Maybe I've finally outgrown second-hand souvenirs. No need to tell that to him.

As I leave the yard sale, I pass the proprietess in her canvas chair. I smile at her, but she returns a scowl. I have nearly reached the street when she catches up to me and roughly grabs my elbow. Squinting into the sun over my shoulder, she drops two quarters in the open top of the bag. They clink softly against the statue.

"No need to get carried away," she says.

Other Iowa Short Fiction Award Books

1983 *Heart Failure*, Ivy Goodman
Judge: Alice Adams

1982 *Shiny Objects*, Dianne Benedict
Judge: Raymond Carver

1981 *The Phototropic Woman*, Annabel Thomas
Judge: Doris Grumbach

1980 *Impossible Appetites*, James Fetler
Judge: Francine du Plessix Gray

1979 *Fly Away Home*, Mary Hedin
Judge: John Gardner

1978 *A Nest of Hooks*, Lon Otto
Judge: Stanley Elkin

1977 *The Women in the Mirror*, Pat Carr
Judge: Leonard Michaels

1976 *The Black Velvet Girl*, C. E. Poverman
Judge: Donald Barthelme

1975 *Harry Belten and the Mendelssohn Violin Concerto*, Barry Targan
Judge: George Garrett

1974 *After the First Death, There Is No Other*, Natalie L. M. Petesch
Judge: William H. Gass

1973 *The Itinerary of Beggars*, H. E. Francis
Judge: John Hawkes

1972 *The Burning & Other Stories*, Jack Cady
Judge: Joyce Carol Oates

1971 *Old Morals, Small Continents, Darker Times*, Philip O'Connor
Judge: George P. Elliott

1970 *The Beach Umbrella*, Cyrus Colter
Judges: Vance Bourjaily/Kurt Vonnegut